Glenn rea

It was soft ~~and~~ ... ... to be there. "The unsub won't get away with this," he promised and thought, *Or any of his other killings*.

She squeezed his fingers but didn't say anything. Nor did she pull her hand away.

When he parked next to Tisha's truck, Glenn felt like this was a moment in which a display of affection was warranted. At least it felt right to him. He met her eyes squarely and said hotly, "My turn to kiss you. Are you game?"

Holding his gaze, Tisha uttered, "Yes, I'm game. Go for it!"

He did, lifting her chin and putting their mouths together, slightly opening his, for a short kiss that became a long one. Both had to catch their breaths when he pulled away.

In memory of my beloved mother, Marjah Aljean, a devoted lifelong fan of Harlequin romance and romantic suspense novels, who inspired me to excel in my personal and professional lives. To H. Loraine, the true love of my life and very best friend, whose support has been unwavering through the many terrific years together, as well as the many loyal fans of my romance, suspense, mystery and thriller fiction published over the years. Lastly, a nod goes out to my great Harlequin editors, Denise Zaza and Emma Cole, for the wonderful opportunity to lend my literary voice and creative spirit to the Harlequin Intrigue line.

KILLER IN
SHELLVIEW COUNTY

R. BARRI FLOWERS

INTRIGUE

Harlequin®
INTRIGUE™

Recycling programs for this product may not exist in your area.

ISBN-13: 978-1-335-45724-0

Killer in Shellview County

Harlequin Enterprises ULC
22 Adelaide St. West, 41st Floor
Toronto, Ontario M5H 4E3, Canada
www.Harlequin.com

Printed in Lithuania

MIX
Paper | Supporting responsible forestry
FSC® C021394

R. Barri Flowers is an award-winning author of crime, thriller, mystery and romance fiction featuring three-dimensional protagonists, riveting plots, unexpected twists and turns, and heart-pounding climaxes. With an expertise in true crime, serial killers and characterizing dangerous offenders, he is perfectly suited for the Harlequin Intrigue line. Chemistry and conflict between the hero and heroine, attention to detail and incorporating the very latest advances in criminal investigations are the cornerstones of his romantic suspense fiction. Discover more on popular social networks and Wikipedia.

Books by R. Barri Flowers

Harlequin Intrigue

Bureaus of Investigation Mysteries

Killer in Shellview County

The Lynleys of Law Enforcement

Special Agent Witness
Christmas Lights Killer
Murder in the Blue Ridge Mountains
Cold Murder in Kolton Lake
Campus Killer
Mississippi Manhunt

Hawaii CI

The Big Island Killer
Captured on Kauai
Honolulu Cold Homicide
Danger on Maui

Visit the Author Profile page at Harlequin.com.

CAST OF CHARACTERS

Tisha Fletcher—A game warden in Shellview County, Georgia, who discovers a murdered female in a wildlife management area and, working in concert with a handsome Georgia Bureau of Investigation agent, uncovers a sinister plot by her killer.

Glenn McElligott—GBI special agent on the hunt for a ruthless serial killer targeting victims with names that are derivatives of Patricia. Glenn fears that this places Tisha, the beautiful game warden whom he is falling for, in grave danger and vows to protect her at all costs.

Sherman Galecki—A senior game warden who may be leading a double life as a serial killer hidden in plain view.

Kurt Stewart—GBI special agent who also wants justice and is willing to do whatever it takes to solve the case. But is he hiding something relevant to the case?

Jeanne Rutland—A fashion designer who survived an attack by the serial killer. Can she identify the killer? Or will she be targeted again?

The Shellview County Killer—A cold-blooded villain who murders his victims by ligature strangulation and has set his sights on Tisha to add to his notoriety.

Prologue

The last thing Tris remembered was hiking in the Manikeke Crossing of the wildlife management area in Shellview County, Georgia, on a Wednesday afternoon, hoping to take full advantage of the inviting natural setting during the summertime for some wildlife viewing—such as red-cockaded woodpeckers, gopher tortoises and other endangered or threatened species. Apart from loving nature, including the abundance of longleaf pines, wild orchids and other features of the rich landscape, she welcomed a reprieve from both the overprotective mother she currently lived with, as well as the overzealous, underachieving boyfriend whose house she'd recently moved out of. As far as she was concerned, the relationship had run its course and she just wanted to get on with her life. Maybe even start over in another state altogether. At twenty-five, she still had her best years ahead of her. Hopefully, she would share them with someone who respected what she brought to the table and could offer as much in return, minus all the drama.

But then something totally unexpected happened.

The man that she had run into on the trail, who had seemed friendly enough, turned out to be anything but. Before she could even react, he had whipped out a stun gun and placed it squarely on her upper chest. She quickly lost all control of her mind and body, which twitched uncontrollably. She must have passed out when she'd fallen and hit her head on the ground.

Now awake, with a splitting headache, Tris managed to open her sore blue eyes and take in the surroundings. She was still in virtually the same spot where she had been zapped by the man. But where was he? Her clothes hadn't been removed, so there seemed to be no sexual assault. Why had he attacked her unprovoked?

Tris then remembered that someone had been strangling people in Shellview County for several months now. The press had referred to the perpetrator as the Shellview County Killer. But none of the murders had occurred in or around Manikeke Crossing. Surely the killer would not be so bold as to target someone—her—in broad daylight in a popular area for hikers, hunters and others?

Come to think of it, Tris realized that she had not actually run into anyone else lately while hiking.

No one except for the man who had used the stun gun on her. So where was he? Should she be worried that he might come after her again?

She struggled to get to her feet. *I have to get out of here and go for help*, she thought, while trying to regain her equilibrium and find the right direction to get out of the Manikeke Crossing.

Tris had only taken a few steps when she suddenly heard a noise behind her, indicating that she wasn't alone. She glanced back over her shoulder and saw him. He had a big grin on his face, as though having planned this moment all along, and was getting some sort of perverse thrill in watching her squirm in fear.

With wobbly legs, she tried to make a run for it, but somehow ended up flat on her face. That was when he pounced on her, and she knew there would be no escape from what he had in store for her.

HE HAD PLANNED every step, wanting to leave little to chance. Just like the other times. Seeing the terror in the eyes of his victims was half the battle. The other half was finishing what he set out to do, knowing there was nothing that could stop him. Unfortunately for them, escape was impossible. Not when he was so determined to complete his mission.

But that didn't mean he wasn't above at least giving the target a fighting chance. So he allowed that tiny glimmer of hope for survival to be out there. Only to snatch it away in the blink of an eye, like taking candy from a misbehaving child.

It was time to put an end to this, once and for all. When she was put out of her misery, he would be out of his.

At least for the moment.

He sucked in a deep breath and then ended her life, so that he could celebrate his great victory thereafter.

Chapter One

Tisha Fletcher drove her state-owned black Ford F-150 truck onto the Manikeke Crossing in Shellview County on Friday morning. The wildlife management area was part of her jurisdiction as a game warden first class in the Region 5 Law Enforcement Division of the Georgia Department of Natural Resources, headquartered in Albany, Georgia. She took note of the built-in laptop with computer-aided dispatch system, along with a high-powered radio. Then there was the Glock 43 single-stack, 9mm Luger pistol she carried in a waistband holster as a uniformed officer of the law and for her own protection. She also had a smart-phone-based body camera attached to her shirt.

All part of the daily and necessary equipment for a Georgia Peace Officer Standards and Training Council certified game warden tasked with enforcing environmental, wildlife, and boating state and federal laws; holding violators of these laws accountable; and educating the public on proper and safe use of Georgia's natural resources. Six years ago, she had attended and graduated from the DNR Game Warden Academy in Forsyth, Georgia, gotten married and been assigned to the work section in Shellview County, a mix of rural and urban landscapes in the southwest part of the state.

Now twenty-eight years old, Tisha was a young Korean American widow. Three years ago, her husband, Bradley Fletcher, an environmental technologist, had died suddenly of a massive heart attack at the age of thirty-two, leaving her devastated and alone. They'd seemingly had their whole lives ahead of them. Until they didn't.

Her small hazel eyes glanced at the 14K gold wedding ring on her finger. She had been reluctant to remove it for what it represented, though she had put the worst of that painful chapter in her life behind her, just as Bradley would have wanted. For the most part, Tisha had focused on her work, which she loved, and it paid off in ways she could never have anticipated. At the start of the year, she had received the prestigious Torch Award from the DNR Law Enforcement Division, as a means of encouraging the progress of young game wardens who happened to be current members of the North American Wildlife Enforcement Officers of America.

Tisha smiled at the honor and was certain that her late husband would have been proud of her for picking herself up and finding a way to excel professionally. Romance was a different story. Her romantic life had been pretty much nonexistent for the last three years, as she never seemed to connect seriously with anyone who met the high standards for what she looked for in a man. Maybe she had set the bar too high. Or maybe finding true love was one and done for her.

She pulled her truck into the parking spot next to the black Ford F-150 she knew belonged to Sherman Galecki, a senior game warden, who last year had received his own special recognition by the DNR, being named Game Warden of the Year. They had both been sent to the Manikeke Crossing to collect and study data on local wildlife and their habitat to help determine abundance, distribution and mortality rates, and then formulate strategies to maintain it.

Emerging from her vehicle, Tisha glanced down at her patrol boots and squared the shoulders of her slender, five-seven frame. She tucked an errant strand of her long brunette hair, fashioned in a low bun, behind one ear and watched as Sherman climbed out of his cab. Tall and firm in his uniform, at thirty-five, he had short dark brown hair styled in a burst fade cut and blue eyes behind round glasses. He had recently ended a long-term relationship and seemed to be content right now just playing the field.

Tisha was glad he hadn't tried to hit on her. Though he wasn't too bad on the eyes, Sherman wasn't really her type. Not to say that she was necessarily in the market for starting a relationship with anyone, even though she was single and available, more or less.

"Hey," Sherman said easily, sporting a grin on his oblong face as he met her halfway.

"Hey." She twisted her thin lips. "Sorry I'm a little late. Got stuck finishing up some paperwork involving a boating accident."

"No problem. Just got here myself, after bumping heads with a couple of illegal and intoxicated road hunters."

"Ouch. Hope you've got a hard head," Tisha quipped with a chuckle, though she knew any such investigation could be dangerous. Especially when alcohol or drugs were involved.

"I do. Them, not so much." He laughed. "Let's do this."

"Alright." She headed into the WMA with him, and they collected data together, observing small game in their habitat amid the green ground cover, sand dunes and longleaf pines.

"Why don't we spread out and double our reach," Sherman suggested.

This made perfect sense to Tisha, considering that she often worked alone, which was par for the course for most game wardens. She told him, "Good idea. We can meet back at our trucks and compare notes."

"Sounds like a plan," he agreed. "See you in a bit."

Tisha headed north and through a grove of turkey oak trees and vegetation, while considering the restoration and fire management of the ecosystem. When she neared a hill, something odd caught her eye. What was that?

As she grew closer, Tisha winced when she realized that the object in question was, in fact, a human being.

It became obvious to Tisha, based on the deteriorating condition of the young female lying awkwardly atop some foliage, that she was dead.

Tisha immediately got on her radio and told Sherman the disturbing news. "There's a dead woman lying here on the hill," she said flatly.

"What?" His voice rang with shock, then he said evenly, "Tell me where to find you…"

After giving him her coordinates, Tisha waited for his arrival while standing guard over the clothed body and trying to ascertain if this was an accident, suicide, or foul play. The area was a hot spot for hunters, which could have resulted in an honest and tragic mistake…or even one unbeknownst to the shooter.

Except for the fact that there was no sign that the woman had been shot.

With no blood coming from a wound, Tisha ruled out

stabbing, as far as a deliberate attack. The body didn't seem to have been prey for a wild or bloodthirsty animal, either.

When she heard the sound of footsteps, Tisha turned to see Sherman moving briskly toward her. He furrowed his brow while regarding the dead woman and snorted out an expletive, then said, "Yeah, she's definitely no longer among the living."

"What do you think happened to her?" Tisha asked tensely, having her own suspicions.

"Without contaminating the body or scene by touching anything, judging by the position of her body, if I had to hazard a guess, I'd say she was killed by someone or something…"

"I was thinking the same thing," she told him, "but more likely the *someone* angle."

"Yeah, probably," Sherman agreed, and took out his cell phone. "Better alert the sheriff and get the Georgia Bureau of Investigation medical examiner down here."

"I'll call the latter," Tisha said, lifting her own cell phone from a side pocket.

She reported the news of a dead body to the medical examiner's office. Though all possibilities for the cause of death were on the table, instinct, as well as that some similar corpses discovered over the last six months in the county had been classified as serial homicides, left Tisha fearful that a serial killer may have struck again.

GEORGIA BUREAU OF INVESTIGATION Special Agent Glenn McElligott sat at his L-shaped black espresso-colored wood corner desk in the Region 2 Investigative Office on Beaver Run Road in Midland, Georgia. He was a year removed from his assignment to the Region 12 Investigative Office in Eastman, in Dodge County. As deep gray eyes perused information on his laptop regarding the latest case involving a serial killer prowling the streets of Shellview County, one of several counties within his present jurisdiction, Glenn was tempted to say he was getting too damn old for this.

But having just turned thirty-two, he was hardly ready to check himself into the senior living facility that wasn't too far from his property in the county, in the town of Akerston Heights. Hell, if he was being honest about it, he would admit that being a GBI agent was right for him and something he took pride in. After all, he'd been at this for nearly a decade now, becoming a certified Georgia peace officer upon passing the special agent exam and successfully completing the 16-week GBI basic agent course at the Georgia Public Safety Training Center in Forsyth. Before that, he had received his bachelor's degree in criminal justice and criminology from Georgia Southern University's Armstrong Campus in Savannah.

Through the years, Glenn had been involved in his fair share of tough investigations, dealing with a wide array of criminal activity: mass murders, missing person cases, sex offenses, human trafficking, cold cases, and more. But his latest assignment was every bit as unsettling and perhaps even more mystifying. Someone was strangling people to death—female and male victims—and leaving the corpses in both plain view and less visible spots throughout the county. So far, three people had been murdered in the past six months and they were linked to one unsub, whom the local press had given the moniker the Shellview County Killer.

So far, no identifiable DNA or prints and no reliable info on a physical description of the perpetrator had surfaced. The modus operandi was ligature strangulation of the unsub's victims, while doing so brazenly, and had proven quite elusive. This frustrated Glenn, even though he was certain it was only a matter of time before the killer's luck ran out and the perp was locked up where such offenders belonged for the rest of their miserable lives.

That can't happen soon enough, Glenn told himself keenly, running a hand through his short dark hair. No one else had to die. At least that was his fervent hope. When in college, a friend had gotten into a barroom brawl, only to be strangled to death by a jealous boyfriend. Glenn wouldn't wish that kind of attack on anyone. Least of all some innocent people who were apparently being randomly targeted by a serial killer.

When his cell phone buzzed, Glenn, in his short-sleeved, flex collar blue shirt, turned and grabbed the phone. He saw that the call was coming from the Shellview County Sheriff's Department.

This can't be good, Glenn thought, sensing as much given the timing, as he answered routinely, "Agent McElligott." He listened as he was told about the discovery of a dead female in the Manikeke Crossing on Foxx Road. The circumstances of the death were described as suspicious. "I'm on my way," he said, after taking down the GPS coordinates.

Glenn rose to his full six feet, three inches height. He had a SIG Sauer P320-M18 modular handgun system 9mm Luger sidearm inside a leather pocket holster on his slacks, along with a Taser. Just as he was about to brief the special agent in charge, she stepped into his corner office.

Rhianna Kingsley was African American, in her early forties and around five-ten with a medium frame. She had blond hair in a curly bob and was frowning as her brown eyes gazed at him. "I take it you heard about the body found in the Manikeke Crossing?"

"Yeah, just got off the phone with the sheriff's department," he confirmed bleakly. "I'm headed over there right now."

"Good. Our crime scene specialists will meet you at the wildlife management area."

"Okay." Glenn paused, reading her thoughts about the worst-case scenario, which in this instance was more evidence of a serial killer at work. "I won't jump to any conclusions," he offered. "Maybe this will turn out to be something that won't necessarily require the assistance of the GBI."

"One can only hope," Rhianna said. "We certainly have enough other investigations on our hands, including the one you're working on now. We don't need any more bodies to have to deal with in the process."

"I agree." He paused thoughtfully. "Only one way to find out."

She lowered her chin. "Don't let me stop you, Agent McElligott."

Glenn nodded. Shortly, he was out the door and into his black Dodge Durango Pursuit SUV. It was equipped with an AR-15 semiautomatic rifle as backup firepower, if needed in the course of his duties.

During the drive, he considered that the independent GBI's assistance had been requested in what turned into a serial killer investigation, with him taking the lead in trying to solve the case, while at the same time fully cooperating with the sheriff's department in the pursuit of justice for the victims.

After arriving at the Manikeke Crossing, Glenn flashed his identification in what had clearly become a bona fide crime scene, with the yellow tape cordoning off the area in question. He got the general sense that the situation would likely get worse before things got better. This was confirmed, more or less, as he conferred with the GBI crime scene specialists, who had already begun to process the immediate surroundings.

He made his way farther inside the WMA and approached the sheriff, who was talking with two game wardens—one male, the other female. The three turned Glenn's way in unison. Shellview County Sheriff Marjorie Pierce, of medium build and in full uniform, was in her fifties, with green eyes and crimson hair in a pixie cut. Glenn was glad to be able to assist in this investigation that was within her jurisdiction, having worked together before on a joint task force involving sex trafficking in the state.

"Sheriff Pierce," Glenn said in a friendly but ill-at-ease tone, "I got the call about a dead body found…"

Marjorie nodded dourly. "Unfortunately, that's what we're looking at."

He gazed at the male game warden, who was about his height and build, and said, "GBI Special Agent Glenn McElligott."

"Sherman Galecki," the game warden introduced himself.

"Nice to meet you." Glenn shook his hand with a firm grip and eyed the female game warden.

"Tisha Fletcher," she said, her tone even.

It took only a moment to assess the attractive game warden. She had pretty hazel eyes and her brunette hair was obviously long and pulled up from her heart-shaped face into a bun, with curtain bangs. Even in uniform, he could see that she was well-proportioned on a slender frame.

"Hello," Glenn said respectfully, and stretched out his long arm to shake her hand. He couldn't help but notice the wedding band on her other hand and told himself that her husband was a lucky man. Something that Glenn had thus far found himself falling short on—though not from lack of trying. He wanted to meet someone who was marriage material and a person he could grow with.

They released hands and Marjorie said, "Warden Fletcher is the one who found the body."

Glenn eyed the game warden again and asked, "Where?"

"Just up this hill," she responded, and began to lead the way. "Sherman and I were collecting data in different parts of the WMA, when I spotted her lying on and partially covered by some underbrush…"

When they arrived at the spot, Glenn bent down and studied the deceased female. She was slender and had medium-length light blond hair tied in a ponytail. He guessed that she was in her late twenties to early thirties. She was lying on her side, wearing a carrot-colored cropped tank top, black high-waist leggings and white sneakers. It seemed apparent to him by her pallid coloring that she had been dead for more than a day. He noted the discoloration around her neck, suggesting she could have been strangled. Furthermore, there appeared to be two small puncture wounds on the part of her chest that was exposed, consistent with use of a stun gun.

"And this is exactly the way she was found?" he asked, having no reason to believe either game warden would have tried to move the body, potentially corrupting evidence of a crime.

"Yes," Tisha assured him. "We had no desire to complicate the investigation in any way."

Sherman backed her up on this. "Once Tisha alerted me as to what she'd found, I came over and we both inspected the dead woman without touching her."

"Just checking," Glenn said, regretting putting the two on the spot, knowing they were all on the same team. "Judging by her attire, it appears that she was hiking or jogging, before something happened—"

"So what do you think we're looking at here?" Sheriff Pierce asked urgently.

Glenn understood by her expression that she was cutting to the chase as it related to the possibility that the deceased was another victim of a serial killer.

"Could this be the work of the so-called Shellview County Killer?" Tisha asked bluntly, with unease, before he could respond to the sheriff.

"Well, without getting ahead of ourselves," he answered coolly, "and pending an autopsy, it appears that she was accosted by someone, who either came with her or followed her into the Manikeke Crossing, or she ran into by chance, such as a hunter…"

"If a hunter did this, we should be able to narrow down some possibilities based on hunting licenses issued for hunting on this WMA," Sherman stated.

"That would help," Glenn said, while considering that the unsub serial killer could be a hunter as well. "Do we know the name of the dead woman?"

"Not yet," the sheriff said sadly. "Appears her identification is missing. Assuming she came here alone and ran into harm's way, it was either left behind or taken by her killer—"

"We'll need to identify her as soon as possible," he stressed, knowing that this could be a key factor in the circumstances that led to her death.

"As part of the DNR Law Enforcement Division," Tisha said, "whatever we can do to assist in the investigation, Agent McElligott and Sheriff Pierce, just let us know."

Glenn could tell by her tone that she was as eager to see this death solved, occurring where it did, as he was, giving him a certain sense of anticipation of them working together toward a common goal. Sherman seconded this.

"Okay," Glenn responded. The sheriff also welcomed their cooperation.

Signaling for the crime scene technicians to begin working the area around the body before the medical examiner arrived, Glenn instructed that they use a Leica C10 laser scanner for a three-dimensional scan of the crime scene and how it may have been used as a death trap for the hiker or jogger.

The hard part, Glenn knew, was to put these pieces together to make a case for what likely was a murder of the as-yet unidentified victim, who had undoubtedly been in the wrong place at the worst possible time before her death.

Chapter Two

Tisha wondered if she had gone overboard in stating the obvious to the GBI special agent, along with the sheriff, in volunteering assistance in what would almost certainly be a homicide investigation. After all, the woman's death had occurred within a DNR wildlife-management-area work section. Not to mention, after having discovered the body, Tisha felt it was incumbent upon her to see this through to its conclusion to the extent possible in her position as a game warden, her regular duties and life away from work notwithstanding.

She gazed at Glenn McElligott as he orchestrated the movements by the GBI crime scene investigators in combing the area to collect evidence. Tall and in his early thirties, with jet-black textured hair in a stylish undercut, arresting gray eyes, and in really good shape, Tisha couldn't help but think that the good-looking, square-jawed special agent with a five-o'clock shadow was totally her type. Or at least she felt he could be if the situation presented itself, since she was a widow, too long without real companionship, and wanted to believe someone else might still be out there for her in this world.

Dream on, Tisha told herself, as she let the thought pass and got back to the moment at hand, while watching the associate medical examiner and his team arrive and take possession of the decedent, with an autopsy forthcoming to determine the manner and circumstances of what had already been classified as a suspicious death.

Tisha could only wonder if a serial killer had made his way to the Manikeke Crossing to cause trouble in a major way. When the dust settled and everyone had begun to clear out from the main crime scene, she found herself being approached by Agent McElligott.

"You have a cell phone?" he asked.

She batted her eyes and quipped, "Doesn't everyone?"

"Can I see yours?" he asked with a straight face, even as Tisha removed the phone from her pocket and handed it to him. She watched as he put in his cell phone number and said, "In case you happen to come upon anything relevant to this investigation, feel free to call me anytime…"

"Will do," she promised, and sent him her own cell phone number should he wish to contact her pertaining to the case. Or maybe he might want it someday outside of the investigation. Who knew?

"Thanks." He gave a crooked little grin and walked away, meeting up with Sheriff Pierce and some of her deputies.

A few minutes later, Tisha had walked back to the parking lot with Sherman, where their Ford F-150 trucks awaited them.

"Been a hell of a way to start our day," he moaned.

She sighed. "Tell me about it."

Sherman eyed her. "You going to be okay?"

"Not like I have much of a choice," Tisha answered truthfully. After all, as an armed game warden, she had to be up to the task of dealing with whatever—or whomever—she encountered. That included dead bodies. Didn't mean she had to be comfortable with it. "I'm sure that Agent McElligott and the sheriff's department will get to the bottom of the poor woman's death, whether it's tied to a serial killer or not."

"Yeah, one can only hope. We don't need that type of trouble while doing our jobs." He touched his glasses and headed for his truck.

"Catch you later," she called out to him and got into her own cab. There, Tisha watched Sherman drive off, then she got out her cell phone to give an update on the latest happenings to the work section boss, Sergeant Fritz Alvarez.

When his full face appeared on the small video screen, surrounded by black hair in an Edgar cut, Tisha followed up on their earlier chat. "The GBI is looking into the suspicious death of the female hiker, which appears to be homicide."

Tisha could see the intensity in his deep brown eyes as Fritz, in his midforties, said, "Sorry you had to be put through that, and sorrier about the hiker."

"Me, too," Tisha commented, covering both fronts.

"Do they know who the victim is yet?"

"No, they're still trying to identify her." She could only imagine the heartbreak of the woman's family or close friends, upon learning what would be unthinkable for most people. Until it happened.

"Well, I'm sure the authorities will get to the bottom of it," Fritz said.

"Hope so." Tisha took a breath, fearing they might not like what they discover, if in fact the death could be tied to a serial murderer.

"Sherman was shaken up by it, too," the sergeant remarked. "No matter your toughness, this type of encounter never goes down easily."

"No, it doesn't," she admitted.

"Unfortunately, it can come with the territory, which, in this case, is the entire county."

Tisha met his gaze knowingly. "We'll get through it."

"I know you will," Fritz said confidently. "In the meantime, we'll certainly step up our patrols of the hot spots within our jurisdiction, which, if nothing else, will hopefully help give visitors some added peace of mind."

"That will be good."

"Yeah."

"Well, I better get back to work," she told him, neither requesting nor expecting to be given time off to come to terms with the trauma of finding a dead body. That would need to work itself out on its own schedule.

After disconnecting, Tisha started the truck and headed out. She thought briefly about Agent Glenn McElligott, wondering what he could discover about the dead woman. And what might remain unknown. That would be for him to determine. Along with the other aspects of his investigation, over and beyond his personal life, however that played into working for the GBI.

GLENN WAS ALREADY on his way home for the day when word came in that the dead woman had been tentatively identified. According to a member of his crime scene investigators, the driver's license and cell phone belonging to a Tris Lindberg had been found scattered in undergrowth just outside the crime scene. Now, this information needed to be confirmed by the sheriff's department, along with getting the results of the autopsy, in piecing together a timeline and exact cause of death.

I have a very bad feeling that the Shellview County Killer has struck again, Glenn told himself bleakly. But he knew he couldn't get ahead of himself just yet in this investigation. Whatever the case, a woman was dead, and someone needed to be held accountable.

He pulled his SUV into the driveway of his two-story, three-bedroom custom home on Fennly Street. It sat on forty acres of rolling hills and mature pine trees, not far from Lake Oliver. He had purchased the fenced property after being reassigned to the area a year ago. It had pretty much everything he wanted in a residence, other than perhaps a human companion to share his life with. He held out hope that could still happen for him as a healthy man with a lot of loving to give to the right woman.

The instant he stepped inside the house, Glenn was practically bowled over by his lovable black Labrador retriever named Riley, whom he'd had for three years now.

"Hey, boy. It hasn't been that long since I left for work," Glenn told him with a chuckle, while petting the dog's head. "Love you, too, Riley."

He played with the dog for a bit, then let him go. Riley ran across the hand-scraped, engineered hardwood flooring, into the U-shaped kitchen and back out, disappearing down the hall.

Glenn glanced around the open-concept first floor with its picture windows with vertical blinds and relaxed modern furnishings. After heading up the winder staircase, he put away his firearm safely and freshened up while trying to decide what to have for dinner.

Back downstairs, Glenn fed Riley some dry dog food, then decided to have leftover cheese and pepperoni pizza, washing it down with beer as he ate standing up.

Once done, he settled onto the midcentury-modern armchair in the great room, where, with Riley lying at his feet, Glenn grabbed his acoustic guitar and started to play. Ever since his parents had gotten him a guitar at ten years of age, playing the instrument had been one of his favorite pastimes. As well as a means to relieve some of the stress that life brought.

He thought about his current investigation. At the moment, that was the death of Tris Lindberg. Had someone targeted her in particular? Did she know or recognize her attacker?

If only she could speak from the grave, it would save me from needing to speak on her behalf in nailing her killer, Glenn told himself. His thoughts gravitated to the pretty game warden who discovered the body, bringing it to his attention.

He wondered if coming upon the victim would leave a lasting impact on her. Or had she hardened her ability to deal with such incidents by virtue of a law enforcement profession that required toughness and fortitude?

Something told him that she would want to be kept in the loop on how this case unfolded, seeing that the game warden had been inadvertently drawn into the murder investigation. He was more than happy to oblige her from one professional to another...while knowing that on a personal level, as a married woman there were no possibilities that his attraction to her would go any further than appreciating her from a safe distance.

SHELLVIEW COUNTY SHERIFF Marjorie Pierce hated this part of her job—the part where she had to notify one or more family members of a murder victim that the person was

dead. And, as such, would not be showing up for breakfast, lunch, dinner, or whatever, again. But unfortunately,
this was par for the course. Someone had to be the bearer
of bad—make that very bad—news.

That would be her.

She got comfortable behind the wheel of her black Ford
Explorer SUV and headed out to the address on Millburn
Lane in the county town of Breyford, where Marjorie had
been told that Tris Lindberg lived off and on with her
mother, Alyssa Lindberg. Or at least she used to when
still among the living.

It struck Marjorie to the core when she thought of her
own daughter, Sarah, who wasn't much younger than the
victim. She could only imagine how it would tear her
up inside were Sarah to lose her life in such a tragic and
senseless way. Having raised her on her own, by and large,
as a divorcée, she wanted her daughter to have everything
in life she deserved. That included attending Princeton
University, where Sarah was in graduate school and working on her PhD in electrical and computer engineering.
Pity that Tris Lindberg was destined to never be afforded
that same courtesy in living out her dreams.

When Marjorie reached the ranch-style house, she
parked along the curb, then headed up to the door, past
a red Honda Accord in the driveway. It took a couple of
rings of the doorbell before the door opened.

Marjorie looked into the face of a petite, fortysomething woman with short brown and gray hair, and said
to her, "I'm Sheriff Pierce. Are you Alyssa Lindberg?"

"Yes," she responded, seeming ill at ease. "How can I
help you, Sheriff?"

Marjorie waited a beat, before she responded in the

only way she knew how, and that was to get right to the heart of the matter. "I'm afraid I have some bad news… It's about your daughter—"

AFTER HER SHIFT ENDED, Tisha drove to Blair Bay, where she lived in a two-bedroom town house on Tallins Drive, near the Chattahoochee River. She had moved there shortly after her husband's death, knowing she couldn't bear to continue living in the Georgian cottage they shared. She opted instead for a fresh start.

Or at least to give herself a chance to recalibrate her life and see what else—and maybe who else—was out there for her.

Glenn McElligott entered her head, but Tisha quickly let the thought slide. The truth was that she knew far too little about the good-looking special agent to get too carried away by his appearance and the few words that had passed between them. If they ever got the chance to really talk, and he was available, too, well, who knew where it could lead.

She reached her place and used the remote to open the attached garage with an entryway into the corner two-story unit that sat beside a cluster of pink flowering dogwood trees. After driving inside, she closed the garage and left the car.

Before even heading into the town house, Tisha could hear her dog, Jacky, barking in anticipation of seeing her.

Back at you, she thought, as Tisha went in and greeted the German shepherd warmly. She had inherited, more or less, the ten-year-old retired DNR Law Enforcement Division K-9 Unit dog, after his handler had been given a younger partner to fight crime.

Tisha considered the two of them to be a good fit in fighting off each other's loneliness. She watched as Jacky licked her hand playfully, and Tisha wondered if the dog was eager to be let out into the big fenced-in backyard for some exercise.

Instead, Jacky abruptly scurried away from her, across the bamboo flooring, past rustic furnishings and large windows with faux wood blinds in the spacious living-and-dining-room combo, and up the stairway to the second floor.

I'll be up shortly, she told herself, and headed into the open kitchen with its granite countertops and black stainless-steel appliances. She took a goblet out of the wood cabinet, opened the fridge, removed a half-filled bottle of red wine and poured it.

After sipping a bit of wine, Tisha filled a dog bowl with chicken-and-white-rice dog food for Jacky, and then got out some leftover tuna noodle casserole to microwave for herself.

As if sensing dinner was about to be served, Jacky came back downstairs and went right to her meal.

Tisha smiled and went upstairs, where she put her firearm away and changed into more comfortable clothing— a yellow T-shirt and brown shorts. She washed her face and let down her hair, which fell below her shoulders.

Twenty minutes later, she was sitting barefoot in a wood-ladder side chair at the round pedestal dining table, eating alone once again. She wondered if this would change anytime soon. Or was this destined to be the story of her life, whether she wished to move forward or not, in longing for human companionship, taking nothing away from her lovable former K-9 dog.

THE FOLLOWING MORNING, after taking Jacky out, Tisha drove to work, patrolling Shellview County rural areas for any violations pertaining to wildlife, waste and litter laws. She couldn't help but think about yesterday's unfortunate turn of events and the sad reality of how one wrong move in life could ruin it forever, as was the case for the dead female hiker.

Just as Tisha was about to check in with Sherman, to see if he, too, had to come to grips with what went down at the Manikeke Crossing, her cell phone rang. She saw that the caller was Agent McElligott and that immediately commanded her attention.

"Hello," she said, putting him on speakerphone.

"Hey. In case you haven't already heard, we've identified the woman you found in the WMA as Tris Lindberg, a twenty-five-year-old from Breyford."

"No, I hadn't been briefed," Tisha confessed, while picking up noise from the road in the background, indicating that he was also in his vehicle.

"Well, I thought you ought to know."

"Thanks for the update. Have you learned anything else about her that's pertinent to the investigation?"

"Well, apart from being the apparent victim of foul play, Ms. Lindberg may well have been targeted…" he said, leaving it at that.

Tisha sighed, though wasn't really surprised, in remembering the signs that suggested as much. "I'm sorry for her," she said nonetheless.

"Me, too."

She couldn't help but wonder if he had connected this to the serial killer case.

Glenn cut into Tisha's thoughts when he uttered, "In any

event, I'll be giving a full briefing on the death at eleven thirty this morning at the sheriff's department. If you'd like to attend, given your involvement in discovering the victim, you're welcome to. Same with Sherman Galecki."

"Yes, I would definitely like to be there." She suspected the same would be true for Sherman, who may as well have found the body himself, seeing that they had both been collecting data in the same area.

"Good..." The GBI special agent paused, as if wanting to say something else to her, but had a change of heart, then simply replied, "I'll see you then."

"Okay." Tisha disconnected, eager to hear what he had to say and, truthfully, keen to see him again, while uneasy at the same time, as she anticipated the murder would be linked to several others in recent months who had died in a similar fashion.

She gave Sherman a buzz and he quickly said, "Heard the victim has been identified and that she was killed by someone."

"Yes, sadly."

"Agent McElligott invited us to his joint update with Sheriff Pierce," Sherman noted.

"I just spoke to him," Tisha confirmed. "Are you going?"

"Yeah. Maybe we'll get some more definitive answers as to why this happened in one of our WMAs and whether or not we need to be on the serious lookout for a killer..."

"I agree." She hung up, thoughtful, before touching base with Fritz Alvarez about the status of the investigation.

Chapter Three

Glenn had to admit that he liked the sound of Tisha Fletcher's voice when he heard it again. Or was even that stepping over the line when talking about a married woman? Why should it be? No harm in admiring a pleasant-sounding voice. Or even an attractive face with a nice body—from what he could interpret of the game warden in full uniform—for that matter.

The important thing was that she and Sherman Galecki deserved to know what they had learned thus far about the dead female Tisha had come upon.

Glenn believed he would have more answers about the death of Tris Lindberg at the briefing today and, very likely, some connecting of dots to the broader serial-killer investigation.

He pulled up to the Georgia Bureau of Investigation's medical examiner's regional laboratory on Deckler Street in Shellview County, where the autopsy on the victim had taken place this morning.

After stepping inside the building and flashing his ID, Glenn made his way to the lab, where the associate medical examiner, Dr. Ned Karakawa, was on his cell phone, but waved him over.

In his early sixties, Dr. Karakawa was lean and had

short white hair in a quiff style. He had on brown rectangle eyeglasses, a stained white lab coat and latex gloves. While waiting for him to end the phone chat, Glenn glanced at the nearby autopsy table, where Tris Lindberg's corpse was covered by a sheet up to her neck.

"Agent McElligott…" the associate medical examiner got his attention after hanging up.

Glenn regarded him with a nod. "Dr. Karakawa."

"Sorry, didn't mean to keep you waiting."

"No problem." Glenn cut to the chase. "What can you tell me about the death of Tris Lindberg?"

Karakawa touched his glasses and frowned. "Well, it wasn't pretty. As I indicated in the preliminary report and have now confirmed, Ms. Lindberg died of ligature strangulation from what appears to be some type of thin cotton cord," he said matter-of-factly. "I'm ruling the death a homicide."

Glenn muttered a sound of resignation and then asked, to be sure in his suspicions, "What about the injuries to her chest?"

Karakawa moved over to the body and slid the sheet down to her chest, pointing at the marks. "Similar to recent postmortems, these puncture wounds indicate that the decedent was subjected to some kind of stun gun, making it easier for whoever killed her to gain complete control, before finishing her off."

"How long was she dead?" Glenn questioned.

"I'd say anywhere from twenty-four to thirty-six hours or so."

Glenn mused about that. "Any chance she could have been killed elsewhere and the body dumped where it was found?"

"There's always a chance," the associate medical examiner replied. "But given the rather steep and dense location, and good possibility of detection were that to have occurred, I'd say the decedent was almost certainly killed close to where she was found."

"I agree." Glenn eyed the victim again, almost feeling the pain she must have endured both physically and psychologically from her ordeal. "Were there any signs of a sexual assault?"

Karakawa shook his head. "Not that I could detect."

"Just thought I'd ask." Glenn was pensive, before he asked curiously, "Could this be an isolated incident?" *Or, in other words, unrelated to the serial killings?* he thought.

Karakawa sighed. "I'll leave that for you and the sheriff's department to determine, Agent McElligott." He paused thoughtfully. "That being said, after conducting this postmortem examination, the particulars of the homicidal death in relation to the aforementioned murders make me believe it's unlikely to be an isolated attack. Simply put, the murders were much more likely to have been committed by the same person."

"My sentiments exactly," Glenn said soberly, while getting what he needed from the associate medical examiner, in linking the murder to a serial killer.

TISHA FINISHED HER morning rounds by citing three minors who were caught drinking alcohol near Lake Oliver. She hoped, but doubted, that they would heed this moment as a predictor of future trouble, should they continue down a path that could well escalate into more serious problems.

She drove up to the Shellview County Sheriff's Department on Twelfth Street in Blair Bay and parked in the lot, then headed inside to get the scoop on the death of Tris Lindberg and its relationship, if any, to other deaths that occurred in the county in recent months.

The briefing was held in a conference room on the first floor. Inside, as members of law enforcement stood around, Tisha spotted Sherman, who had beaten her there and was chatting away flirtatiously with a pretty blond-haired deputy. *Good for him*, Tisha thought, while not knowing if he was actually hitting on the deputy or not.

"Hey." She heard a voice from behind and turned to gaze into the sharp eyes of Glenn McElligott.

Tisha grinned softly. "Agent McElligott."

"Feel free to call me Glenn, Warden Fletcher," he said smoothly, and as an obvious move to reduce the formalities both ways.

She happily took the bait and responded accordingly. "Only if you'll call me Tisha."

He flashed straight, white teeth. "Deal."

"So where do things stand in the investigation?" she asked, suspecting what his answer might be.

"Well, we're about to give an update," Glenn told her. "Afterward, if you have any further questions, I'll be happy to answer them."

"Fair enough." She smiled at him and watched as he headed toward a podium, joining Sheriff Pierce.

Tisha listened as the sheriff was all business in laying out the case in general terms for what was believed to be a strangulation-style serial killer in their midst, with Tris Lindberg as the latest victim.

GLENN WAS ALL ears as Sheriff Marjorie Pierce gave the foundation for their joint effort and paved the way for him to spell out the specifics of the case. He glanced at Tisha, wondering if she was up for hearing some of the unsettling details. The game warden had likely seen her fair share of criminal activity within her territory. But he suspected that serial murder was not amongst the criminality she encountered. Didn't mean, though, that Tisha would shy away from having a better handle on the circumstances involving the homicide victim she'd happened to come upon.

Marjorie was finishing her briefing in a somber tone of voice. "We're all in this together. We'll do whatever it takes to crack this nightmare case and make Shellview County a safe place to live and visit again..."

When Glenn took to the podium, he didn't mince words in getting to the heart of the matter. "We're almost certainly looking at a serial killer on the prowl, who the press has given the moniker the Shellview County Killer. I'm sure they're seeking to dramatize it, borrowing from other notorious serial killers' names, such as Jack the Ripper, Boston Strangler and Green River Killer. What we can ascertain, whatever the unsub's handle, is that he seemingly has no qualms about targeting the growing number of victims, which currently stands at four. All of them died from ligature strangulation in different locations and were subdued by the perpetrator with the help of a stun gun."

Holding a stylus pen, Glenn turned toward a large touch-screen display and brought up a split-screen image of the first victim. One image was of the victim still very much alive, and the other was as seen when the remains were discovered.

"Patsy Dunnock, a twenty-seven-year-old African American hairstylist and part-time model, was found strangled to death six months ago inside her white Acura Integra that was parked outside her apartment on Keblan Avenue in Akerston Heights. The killer had apparently been hiding in the back seat and caught her by surprise."

Glenn took a moment to look at the victim's attractive oval face with big brown eyes. It was surrounded by long and curly hair in a pink-to-copper-ombré style, parted on the right side. He allowed the stark living image to sink in before moving on to the second and third victims.

"Walt Patrick, an IT manager, age thirty-four, and his girlfriend, twenty-nine-year-old artist Patti Arnaz, were found strangled to death three months ago at Brenner Park in Nelse's Creek."

Glenn put their pictures on the screen, before disaster struck the nice-looking couple. Patrick, who was white, had dark hair in a buzz cut and blue eyes. Arnaz, Hispanic, had brown eyes and wore her brown hair with blond highlights in a spiky style. Glenn switched to the harsh but necessary corpse images of the pair from the morgue. "This is what became of them," he muttered, and then replaced it with the split screen of before and after images of the homicide victims.

Lastly, he put up the split-screen images of the most recent victim of the serial killer, and said sourly, "Yesterday, the body of twenty-five-year-old Tris Lindberg was discovered by game wardens at the Manikeke Crossing." Glenn regarded her attractive face, with blue eyes and long blond hair with retro bangs. He glanced at the picture of her corpse and then eyed Tisha, knowing that reliving the moment of discovery couldn't have been easy. But she had wanted to be here, to catch the briefing. "The bank teller was apparently hiking when the unsub used a stun gun to subdue and then strangle her. According to the associate medical examiner, the victim had been left there by her killer for as long as thirty-six hours, before the crime came to light."

Glenn turned off the monitor to spare them any unnecessary discomfort in viewing, then continued, "That makes three women and one man that we believe were victims of the so-called Shellview County Killer. Surveillance video was able to pick up a tall and slender white male with short dark hair, either leaving or in the vicinity of some of the crimes around the time they occurred. As of yet, we haven't been able to get much more than a general description and guesstimate his age range at anywhere from early thirties to midforties. No reliable DNA or prints have been collected and no witnesses have surfaced to pinpoint the unsub's identity. Nor have we been able to lock down a solid motive or connection between the victims. The current thinking is that the unsub targeted the females—perhaps randomly or intentionally— and the male victim was there by happenstance or simply in the way when going after the intended target."

Glenn sighed with frustration but refused to affix blame on the sheriff's department investigators, or himself, for that matter. They were all doing their respective jobs to the best of their abilities, as would be expected. Still, he knew that as the GBI special agent assigned to the case, he needed to find the serial killer and expose him for all the world to see. Then make sure that he was held accountable to the fullest extent of the law for what he'd done.

TISHA LISTENED WITH interest and sadness as Glenn linked the death of Tris Lindberg to a serial killer. Though this had been expected, all things considered, it was still a blow to think that Tris had been murdered in a wildlife management area that fell within Tisha's jurisdiction. That hadn't been the case for the earlier murders attributed to the Shellview County Killer, but it was no less unsettling. One murder within her territory as a game warden was one homicide too many.

I'd like to get more insight into the investigation, she told herself sincerely, if only for her own peace of mind, while the case went on. Not to mention, it would help her to be on the lookout for any other threats that could present themselves in the course of her work from the at-large serial killer.

"So what do you think?" Sherman asked as he walked up to her, snapping her out of her reverie as the briefing was ending.

Tisha met his curious gaze while wondering if he had gotten the number of the cute deputy he had been talking with. "I think we need to be vigilant in our duties while the killer's out there," she replied flatly.

"Aren't we always?" he queried. "We handle all types of law violators. This isn't any different, other than the fact that he's probably hidden in plain view and is, more likely than not, looking for soft targets that he can get the jump on, and out of the reach of game wardens, for the most part."

She couldn't help but chuckle. "I'd say that makes it just a bit different than the norm, wouldn't you?"

"Yeah, I suppose it does." He laughed. "We'll keep our eyes open for anyone acting suspicious."

"That's a good idea," Glenn said as he approached them.

Tisha smiled at him. "Hey. Thanks for giving us an update."

"Happy to do so." He grinned evenly.

"Hope you get this bastard soon," Sherman stated.

"You and me both," Glenn assured him. "We're working on that but can always use any help we can get."

Sherman nodded. "If anything draws our attention, you'll be the first to know."

"Good." Glenn patted his broad shoulder.

"If you'll excuse me, I'd like to have a word with Sheriff Pierce," Sherman said, and gazed at Tisha. "See you when I see you."

"Okay," she told him, and turned to Glenn, offering him a nervous smile.

He smiled back and said, "So do you have any questions?"

Tisha thought about it for a moment or two, before looking him right in the eyes as she responded whimsically, "Would you like to grab a bite to eat?"

"Not exactly what I had in mind." Glenn chuckled. "Uh, sure, I'm down with that. Starved, in fact."

How embarrassing would that have been if he'd turned me down, Tisha told herself, coloring nonetheless. "Cool," she responded, knowing it was lunchtime. She added candidly, for the record, "I do have some questions as well, pertaining to your investigation into Tris Lindberg's murder..."

He nodded. "Alright."

She lifted her chin. "We can take my vehicle."

"Lead the way," he told her.

As they headed outside, their hands touched inadvertently, and Tisha felt a sudden tingling ripple throughout her body. She wondered if he'd felt the same strange sensation. Or was it just her?

GLENN HAD TO admit that the last thing he expected was to be invited to lunch by the striking and married game warden. But then again, there was no harm in wanting to learn more about the investigation over a meal. Especially now that she had been drawn into the case indirectly. He turned in his seat and gazed at her profile for a moment while she drove, then asked curiously, "Where are we going?"

"There's a great place on Batten Avenue called Pauletta's Café that pretty much has everything," she told him.

"I'm familiar with it," he said, having gone there a few times since his transfer. "Good food there."

She smiled. "I agree."

He was curious to know more about her, and asked, "Are you from around here?"

"Depends on what you mean by around," she replied.

"The local area," he clarified.

"I grew up in DeKalb County, Georgia. My parents still live in Stone Mountain there, having emigrated to this country from South Korea before I was born."

Glenn nodded interestedly. "I see."

"What about you?" Tisha asked him. "I'm guessing that you haven't always lived or worked in or around Shellview County?"

"You guessed correctly." He grinned. "Until about a year ago, I was working for the GBI in Eastman. I'm actually from Sandy Springs, Georgia, where my mother and stepfather reside. My dad lives in Topanga, California."

"Cool," she uttered thoughtfully.

He felt the same way in getting some info on her geographical background as another native Georgian and hoped to discover more about the game warden.

Ten minutes later, they were seated in a window booth, where Glenn chose the steak burger and fries off the menu and Tisha went with a turkey BLT sandwich. Both ordered black coffee.

After some brief small talk, she asked him, "Is it possible that Tris Lindberg could have been stalked by her killer, so he knew exactly where she would be when he attacked her?"

Glenn considered what they knew, thus far, about the murder. "That is a possibility," he admitted, biting into a fry, knowing how some stalkers operated by tracking a victim's every movement. "We're looking into every angle to try and piece together Ms. Lindberg's movements in the forty-eight hours before her death to see if there was an indication that someone was stalking her. Or otherwise threatening her. Beyond that, there's also the matter of investigating her death, specifically, with the bigger picture of four deaths in total likely perpetrated by one individual."

Tisha nodded. She bit into her turkey BLT, chewed a bit and wiped her mouth with a napkin—she seemed ill at ease. "It's chilling to think that a serial killer is operating in Shellview County, right under our noses."

"Yeah," he concurred. "No one ever likes to think it can happen where they live. Unfortunately, these things can take place anywhere, at any time. Serial killers tend to pick and choose their killing locations based on wherever they happen to be that provides enough targets to go after, while having cover in one way or another to avoid capture. But the good news is they all slip up, sooner or later, and give us what we need to bring them down."

"That's comforting to know," she said softly. "I just

hope it's sooner than later, so that residents and visitors alike, along with game wardens, can get on with their lives without this specter hanging over us all."

"There's every reason to believe that will be the case. The investigation is ongoing, and we won't stop till we have our man in custody." Glenn tasted his coffee, wishing he could reassure her more. But he understood that the only real remedy for that was to make an arrest, or otherwise stop the unsub from hurting anyone else. He regarded Tisha sipping her coffee and focused especially on her wedding band, which prompted him to ask what had been on his mind. "So how long have you been married?"

Tisha touched her ring self-consciously. "I'm a widow," she informed him. "I lost my husband three years ago to a heart attack."

"I'm sorry to hear that," Glenn uttered, hating to think that she was such a young widow.

"It's o-okay," she said with a stammer, as if to keep him from feeling sorry for her. "It was devastating for sure and came before we could add children to our marriage... But as hard as it's been, I've managed to move on with my life over time." She paused and gazed at the ring. "I've continued to wear it mostly for sentimental reasons and not as an indication that I'm unavailable to anyone."

"I understand." He ate more of his steak burger, while finding himself emboldened in knowing that she was open to romance again should the right person come along.

"How about you?" Tisha asked, getting his attention. "Married? Kids?"

"Not married and no kids," Glenn told her. "But not for lack of want in both instances." He sighed. "I suppose that between the demands of the job and rotten luck in developing a successful relationship, things have yet to work my way in that regard."

"I wouldn't give up on a happy ending," she said, smiling at him over her coffee mug. "You have plenty of time to find who you're looking for. Or be found by her to your mutual satisfaction."

He grinned back, intrigued by her, along with the possibilities that had presented themselves. "I'll keep that in mind."

"So how long have you been with the Georgia Bureau of Investigation?" she asked him.

"In September, it'll be ten years," he said proudly.

"That's a long time." She grinned. "You obviously enjoy what you do."

"Not always. It can be pretty demanding, if not downright frustrating at times, but it does have its rewards." *Meeting an attractive game warden has been one fringe benefit*, Glenn told himself. "How long have you been a game warden?"

"Not quite as long as you've been a GBI special agent." She laughed. "Six years and counting."

"Nice." He grinned sideways, impressed. "It obviously agrees with you."

"Not always, as you put it," she confessed. "But for the most part, it's a great job for a person who loves nature and the outdoors." Her expression became downcast. "At least until yesterday, when I discovered a dead body under the worst possible circumstances."

"I'm sorry you had to go through that," he said candidly. "But I'm sure it will pass with time, as do most things we could do without." He hoped she understood that he was referring to those types of tragedies, in particular. As opposed to losing a husband in the prime of her life and likely his.

"I'm sure you're right," she agreed quietly, "especially once her killer is apprehended and Tris is able to rest in peace…"

Along with the other victims of the unsub, Glenn mused, as he drank coffee and thought about the road ahead in that regard.

When Tisha dropped him off at his own SUV, he told her, in noting that she had insisted on paying for the meal, "Thanks for the lunch."

"Thank you for agreeing to it," she countered with a grin.

"Next time it's on me." He wasn't sure if there would be a next time, but Glenn was definitely open to it, if she was.

"Deal." Tisha flashed her teeth, making it clear to him that she was on board.

Chapter Four

Later that afternoon, Glenn paid a visit to Tris Lindberg's mother, whom she had apparently been living with at the time of her death. He hoped to establish a timeline of her movements in the days prior to being killed.

"GBI Special Agent McElligott," he said, identifying himself to Alyssa Lindberg after her friend Irene Jenkins, a pregnant, thirtysomething, blond-haired woman, invited him inside.

Alyssa stared at him blankly through tearstained blue eyes as the three of them stood in the contemporary furnished living room. Her voice shook as she asked, "Do you have news about who killed my daughter...?"

"We're still investigating what happened to her and who was responsible," he responded honestly. "I need to know when you last saw your daughter."

Alyssa drew a breath, as Irene held her hand supportively. "On Wednesday morning, before I went to work. I own a boutique at the Hubbard Mall."

"I understand that Tris worked at a bank?"

"Yes, the Munroe Bank in Breyford. Wednesday was her off day. She loved to go hiking."

"Did she typically hike alone?" Glenn asked. "Or go with someone?"

"Both," Alyssa declared. "Sometimes it was with friends. I have no idea if she went by herself or not that day."

He gazed at her. "Do you know of anyone who might have wanted to harm your daughter?"

Alyssa stared at the question before answering with a hint of suspicion. "Why don't you ask her ex-boyfriend, Michael Beal? Tris lived with him before moving back home last month after Michael lost his job. They had a volatile relationship. He wasn't happy when she left him." Alyssa pursed her lips. "When she didn't come home that night, I feared that Tris had actually gone back to Michael, having done so before. Now, I'm left to wonder if he might have killed her—"

Glenn contemplated if the ex could have resorted to murder as payback for an ended relationship. It was not at all uncommon in modern times in intimate relationships gone sour, including hiring someone else to do his dirty work. But whether this amounted to serial murder, before and after, was a different matter altogether, though he believed that anything was possible and needed to be checked out.

"Where can I find Beal?" he asked.

Once he was given an address, Glenn left the women, while promising to keep Alyssa Lindberg informed of any new developments.

TISHA FELT HAPPY to get to know Glenn McElligott a bit better. Yes, there was still more to learn both ways, but she liked the idea of seeing if there was anything there that could be developed between them.

Glancing at her ring while driving, she realized that

it could scare off men, making them believe she was either spoken for or unable to let go of the past. She hoped that Glenn now understood that it was neither. And that she was open to pursuing whatever came her way, if the person had the right character and was serious about getting involved.

Was Glenn such a man? She considered that he seemed ready to open his heart to someone who could relate to his focus on his career, while not holding that against him.

We'll see where it goes, if anywhere, Tisha told herself, as she parked her truck near Bartin's Creek. She got out and approached a couple of anglers, who were fishing in a prohibited area. The flaxen curly-haired male and a female with short beet-red hair were in their early twenties and exchanged a passionate kiss before realizing they had company.

"Hey, you two," Tisha said in a serious tone. "Didn't you see the sign? This area is off-limits for fishing."

"Must have missed it," the tall and lanky male said sardonically, his fishing line in the water.

Tisha was not amused. "Excuses, excuses," she said. "This isn't a game."

"We're sorry," the female said, holding her own rod unsteadily. "We just thought this was the perfect location to snag some bass for dinner. Can't you cut us some slack?"

"No can do." Though sympathetic to a point, Tisha wasn't quite enough to let them off the hook, no pun intended. "The rules are meant to be followed. You have to leave here, but not before you're both cited. Then you can find a spot to legally fish."

The male grumbled more than the female, but both took their lumps and moved on, with no fish for their trouble.

Tisha was satisfied that she was back in gear with her normal work as a game warden, even if the ghastly thought of Tris Lindberg's body as she had found it still loomed large. And that would likely continue to be the case. Until her killer was brought to justice.

GLENN LEFT HIS vehicle on Baker Street and approached the bungalow, where he saw a man sitting on the stairs of the front porch, smoking a cigarette. He was in his midthirties and slender, and had long, layered dark hair swept backward.

Glenn walked up to him. "Are you Michael Beal?"

"Yeah. Who are you?"

"GBI Special Agent McElligott." He flashed his identification.

Beal furrowed his brow. "Let me guess—you're here about Tris…?"

"Good guess," Glenn said sarcastically. "I'm investigating her death."

"And I bet you're wondering if I had anything to do with it?"

"The thought had crossed my mind." Glenn peered at him. "Heard that things went south in your relationship, pissing you off…"

"Yeah, we broke up and it bothered me." Beal sucked on the cigarette. "But I got over it."

"Really?" Glenn jutted his chin. "You sure about that?"

"Look, I screwed up and Tris left me." He sighed. "Took me a while, but I realized that we weren't right for each other and moved on."

Glenn wasn't convinced of that and asked pointedly,

"I need to know where you were when your ex-girlfriend was murdered."

"I was here," Beal replied matter-of-factly. "With my new girlfriend…" He called for her to come outside.

Glenn watched as a voluptuous twentysomething African American female with long blond box braids emerged from the house and declared, when asked, "Yeah, we're together." She gave Beal an alibi for the time frame when Tris Lindberg was murdered and went back inside.

Giving him the benefit of the doubt until proven otherwise, Glenn asked Beal, "Did Tris ever indicate any concerns about someone who might have threatened or stalked her?"

Beal took a final drag of his cigarette, tossed the butt on the sidewalk and said thoughtfully, "Not really, but I remember one day last week following her to the bank, just to talk. We never did, but I could swear that I saw some other dude checking her out in the bank. Maybe it was just my imagination. Since we were no longer together, I didn't make a big deal out of it, only to have her accuse me of stalking her, or whatever."

"What did this guy look like?" Glenn asked attentively.

Beal shrugged. "I don't know," he responded. "Just average, I guess."

Glenn frowned. "You need to give me more than that, if you're on the level."

After contemplating, Beal said, "He was white, slender, maybe in his thirties… Oh, yeah, he was wearing a hoodie. Nothing else comes to mind."

Glenn mused about this potential new lead. "He never approached her?"

"Not that I saw."

"I may need you to speak with a sketch artist to describe this man," Glenn advised him, while also hoping that surveillance video from the bank might provide more information on the possible suspect.

"If you think it'll help, no problem." Beal ran a hand across his mouth. "Whoever killed Tris deserves to be put away…"

"That much we can agree on," Glenn said, and added, "I'll need to narrow down the day and time frame in which you saw this person hanging around the bank—"

Beal said he would cooperate and Glenn left him on the porch stairs as he wondered if Tris Lindberg's killer had indeed been stalking her beforehand. And perhaps had done the same for the other victims in getting a handle on their routines prior to attacking them. If so, whom might the Shellview County Killer be setting his sights on now?

TISHA PLAYED WITH Jacky in the backyard after work, feeling that the retired K-9 dog seemed to have boundless energy. She imagined that, if called upon, Jacky would still be able to return to the DNR Law Enforcement Division K-9 Unit and pick up where she left off.

No way, Tisha thought firmly. She had no intention of giving up her endearing and loyal companion. She tossed a ball in the air and watched as Jacky went to fetch it, then brought it back to her on cue.

Not to say that she wouldn't mind having a human mate to fill the void—she longed for the type of affection and intimacy that were sorely missing in her life.

Someone like Glenn McElligott would do nicely, she imagined, were they to ever cross that bridge down the line.

Back inside, Tisha refilled Jacky's water bowl, and then

took a shower, before sitting in an upholstered wingback chair in the living room and turning on her TV, where she caught the local news.

According to the attractive blond-haired anchor, the residents of Shellview County were on edge these days with the string of strangulation murders, the most current of which was the killing of Tris Lindberg. Tisha was surprised when her own name was brought up as the game warden who happened upon the body of the homicide victim.

Not exactly the way I want to be thought of, she told herself, even if the facts were public and the reality of a heinous death something that was unavoidable. But with Glenn and Sheriff Marjorie Pierce seriously on the case, Tisha was confident that justice was right around the corner.

On Sunday morning, she went to the Blair Bay Fitness Center on Ketchan Street for a workout with her friend and neighbor, Jeanne Rutland. Tisha spotted her on a treadmill and waved, then headed her way.

The same age and height as her, the newly divorced, green-eyed fashion designer was attractive and blond, sporting a cute shaggy haircut. More importantly, she was in great shape, as Tisha was herself. She worked hard to maintain her fitness, with group classes that included Pilates, yoga and Zumba.

"Hey," Jeanne greeted spiritedly. Her feet, in black sneakers, were moving briskly, and she was wearing a white tank top and blue joggers.

"Sorry I'm a little late," Tisha told her, knowing it was usually the opposite. "Jacky took longer than normal to relieve herself outside this morning."

"It's cool. I love your dog, so I won't fault her for going at her own pace. Kind of like I'm doing right now," she said with a laugh.

"I'd say you've got a pretty nice pace going there." Tisha smiled and stepped onto the treadmill next to hers. She was dressed in a black sports bra and gray shorts, while wearing rose-colored running shoes. Her hair was in a high ponytail.

"Back at you," Jeanne said, as Tisha had quickly gotten into a comfortable groove, while keeping up with her friend.

"Just making up for lost time," she joked.

No sooner had Tisha begun to work up a good sweat, when Jeanne commented, "I heard your name mentioned on a news update as the game warden who discovered that poor woman in the Manikeke Crossing."

"It's true," Tisha confirmed, wishing that wasn't the case. "It certainly threw me for a loop in what was supposed to be a routine data collection, more or less."

Jeanne frowned. "Must have been awful."

"Yeah, you could say that." Tisha wiped her brow with the back of her hand. "Worse is that her death has been linked to a serial killer…"

Jeanne's eyes popped wide. "The Shellview County Killer?"

"That would be the one," she said sadly.

"Scary." Jeanne caught her breath. "How long is it going to take to get this creep?"

"Your guess is as good as mine." Tisha hated to admit it. "I do know, though, that the Georgia Bureau of Investigation is working hard with the sheriff's department to solve the murders by catching the killer."

"That's good to know, anyway."

Tisha thought about Glenn in that moment. Along with the fact that as long as the unsub remained on the loose, it was anything but business as usual for everyone. "Until then, just be careful in your daily life," she warned her friend, as everyone in Shellview County should be while this was going on.

"I will," Jeanne assured her, while slowing down. "You, too."

Tisha took in the words, knowing that no one was safe from potentially becoming a victim here, with women and men targeted as if equal game for the culprit.

Not even a game warden.

GLENN LET HIS Lab run wild on the property for his daily exercise, before bringing Riley with him to a playground in Akerston Heights on Packlin Road, where he was meeting up with fellow GBI Special Agent Kurt Stewart, to shoot some hoops on a basketball court. The two had met when both had been assigned to the Region 12 investigative office. After his divorce was finalized nearly a year ago, his ex, Dixie, had gotten custody of their two children, Kendra and Mitchell, after having lost another child, Greta, to cancer two years earlier. Kurt had transferred to the Region 6 office in Milledgeville, Georgia. It was close enough to Glenn's neck of the woods that they were able to continue getting together to play basketball, when they each had some free time.

Glenn ordered Riley to sit on the grass next to the court and the dog obeyed, ignoring its instincts to the contrary. "Good boy," he told him, and Glenn turned just in time to catch the basketball that had been thrown his way.

"You've still got the reflexes, McElligott," Kurt said with a chuckle.

"Always." Glenn gazed at the special agent who was two years older than him and maybe an inch taller on a muscular frame. His eyes were blue, and he had dark hair in a faded buzz cut and a dimpled chin. Both were wearing athletic clothing and gym shoes. He tossed the ball back at him and said amusingly, "Let's see what you've got, Stewart—"

The two engaged in some trash talking and physical play, then Kurt asked, "So what's happening with your case…?"

Glenn sighed while shooting the ball and watching as it bounced off the rim. "Still trying to dig through the evidence, or lack thereof, in coming up with a suspect and making an arrest."

Kurt ran down the errant shot. "It's never easy when you're trying to track down someone who by his very nature seems bent on killing and isn't looking to slow down by being captured."

"Tell me about it." Glenn frowned. "We'll get there, though, one way or the other."

"We always do," Kurt agreed, backing him up.

Glenn sensed that he was referring to his own current investigation into illegal gambling, as part of the GBI's commercial gambling unit. "Where are you in your investigation?"

"Making some serious headway," he responded, shooting the ball and making the shot. "I expect that we could be issuing arrest warrants at any time now."

"Good to know," Glenn said, always rooting for his fellow GBI agents, just as they always had his back.

Kurt took the ball from his hands and asked casually, "So what's happening with your love life these days? Any action? Or are you like me since my divorce, stuck in a rut?"

Glenn grinned musingly as he thought about Tisha. "Not exactly in a rut, but maybe on the right track."

"Oh, really?" Kurt's eyes lit up with curiosity. "Who's the lucky woman?"

"I think it'll be up to her to determine whether or not getting to know me is good luck or not."

"Fair enough." Kurt laughed. "Keep me posted and I'll do the same, should someone enter my orbit again…"

"You've got it," Glenn said hopefully, while thinking that the next thing he could do was invite Tisha to dinner and plan on her accepting. After all, it was his turn to pay for a meal. Cooking it as well was a fringe benefit. He scooped up the ball, placed a well-timed elbow to Kurt's chest to clear up some room, then executed a perfect jump shot and watched the ball swoosh through the net.

Chapter Five

On Monday morning, Tisha was on patrol in her F-150 truck, when her cell phone rang. She saw that the caller was Glenn, causing her heart to skip a beat. She wondered if the call was an update on the case. Or perhaps more personal in nature?

She put him on speakerphone and said cheerfully, "Hey there."

"Hey." He paused. "I was wondering if you'd like to come to my place tonight for dinner, if you don't have any other plans. Or tomorrow, if that works better for you…?"

"I have no current plans for tonight's meal," Tisha answered quickly. "So the answer is yes, I'd love to have dinner with you."

"Great. How does six sound?"

"Perfect." She smiled at the thought of having someone cook dinner for her, assuming that was the plan. It was something she hadn't experienced in recent memory, apart from her mother doing it. "Would you like me to bring wine or anything?"

"Not necessary. I think I'll be able to cover all the bases," Glenn assured her.

"Alright."

"I'll text you my address," he said.

"Okay," she told him, and they disconnected. The idea of essentially going on a date excited Tisha, especially with someone she found herself attracted to. But she wouldn't get too carried away with it, for fear of disappointment. Best to see how it went and go from there.

As she contemplated this, a report came in of two gopher tortoises found dead under suspicious circumstances in the Manikeke Crossing WMA. She headed that way, hating the thought of deliberate harm coming to the threatened species. Moreover, she couldn't help but think of the murder victim, Tris Lindberg. Returning to the scene of the crime gave Tisha chill bumps in the middle of the summer.

Get over it, she admonished herself. Whatever ordeal Tris had been put through, her suffering was over now, for better or worse. Besides, wasn't Glenn on the case, in pursuit of justice? As was the sheriff's department. They would solve this case and give Tris and the other victims of this serial killer the lasting peace they so deserved.

When she reached her destination, Tisha found that Sherman was already there, along with another game warden. Bree McDaniels was in her late forties, medium-sized and had a light blond chin-length bob.

Tisha approached the two as they stood, as if on guard, beside the dead gopher tortoises that were lying on the bloodstained ground near a cluster of shrubs. "What have you learned about this?" she asked.

Sherman furrowed his forehead. "Looks like they've both been shot."

Tisha regarded the fallen members of the keystone species—their carapaces were brownish-black—with anger. One of the tortoises was larger than the other and appeared to have been shot at least twice, taking the brunt of the punishment. "Who would do such a horrible thing?" she moaned, knowing that the gopher tortoise had been designated the official state reptile of Georgia.

Bree wrinkled her nose and pursed her lips. "Someone—or more than one person—who was heartless and disgusting!"

"Even worse than that," Sherman grumbled. "But we'll get whoever was responsible."

"We'd better," Tisha insisted. "We can't allow someone to get away with this act, encouraging other sick people to try and emulate it."

"Don't even go there," he said, as if horrified at the thought.

"Wish I didn't have to." As it was, she knew that bad behavior often bred more bad behavior, something they had seen all too often.

Bree leaned down toward the gopher tortoises for a closer look and said, "Between the crime scene analysis, ballistics getting the info on the bullets and firearm used, and help from the public, this definitely won't end well for the perp or perps."

Tisha took that to heart as she made herself turn again toward the victims of the attack, which had come on the heels of the murder of Tris Lindberg. She wondered if there was possibly more than coincidence here.

There, I did it, Glenn thought, patting himself on the back for asking Tisha over for dinner. Better yet, she'd said yes. Now, he could only hope that it was a positive sign that something good was happening between them.

His thoughts turned to the man taken into custody by

the sheriff's department as a person of interest in the murder of Tris Lindberg. Surveillance video at the Munroe Bank, where she worked, was able to zero in on the suspect, subsequently identified as thirty-six-year-old Joseph Nicholson, who was described as a drifter and loner with a history of stalking.

"Nicholson's originally from St. Louis," Marjorie noted, as Glenn stood beside the sheriff looking at the suspect on a video monitor. "He's been in and out of trouble for much of his adult life, though nothing has risen to the level of homicidal behavior. Much less, serial murder. Still, we won't know till we know, one way or the other."

"I agree," Glenn told her. "I'll go talk to him."

She nodded. "Let's just see what Nicholson has to say for himself."

After stepping inside the interrogation room, where the suspect sat silently at a small metal table, Glenn observed him for a quick appraisal. Dressed in tattered clothing, he was slender but not skinny and had dirty and thinning straight brown hair touching his shoulders. Deep furrows were etched across his forehead, and he had wide-spaced blue eyes.

"I'm Agent McElligott," Glenn said evenly to him, while sitting across from him in a black vinyl chair. "I need to ask you a few questions."

Nicholson, who wasn't cuffed, rubbed his nose and said in a raspy voice, "Ask away, but I didn't do anything."

Not convinced on his word alone, Glenn told him, "You were picked up after being seen on a security video appearing to be studying a bank employee named Tris Lindberg."

"So what if I was," he snorted defiantly. "Is that a crime?"

"Yes, stalking is a crime," Glenn pointed out matter-of-factly. "Murder is worse."

Nicholson's eyes popped wide. "What are you trying to say?"

"Ms. Lindberg was found strangled to death Friday morning." Glenn peered across the table. "Right now, you're our only suspect."

Nicholson muttered an expletive. "I didn't know Tris was dead," he claimed thoughtfully. "I had nothing to do with that—"

Glenn leaned forward. "Did you know Ms. Lindberg?"

He paused, then replied unevenly, "Not really... She gave me some money when passing by on the street. That's all."

"Why were you stalking her?" Glenn demanded.

"I wasn't stalking anyone. I just needed some money and followed her to the bank, hoping she would be able to give me a little when she took her break." He rubbed his nose again. "But I decided to look for some elsewhere and so I left. Never saw her again."

Glenn noted that the surveillance video supported the part of his story about leaving the bank on his own. Could he have already tracked Tris's movements, though, including following her on her day off to the Manikeke Crossing?

"What were you doing last Wednesday?" Glenn asked him, to see how he reacted when given some latitude.

Nicholson bit his lower lip. "I was at the shelter on Ninth Street," he said. "Slept most of the time. After that,

I just hung out on the street, bumming money off anyone who would give it."

Glenn knew that it would be easy enough to check out the shelter. Apart from that, as much as he wished that this was the man they were looking for in the murder of the bank teller, he wasn't feeling it. Moreover, it seemed unlikely that Nicholson had the physical stamina for making his way up into the wildlife management area to commit a murder and get away with it. Same was true for pegging him as a serial killer strangling his victims, including an able-bodied male.

Still, Glenn asked the suspect about the serial crimes, anyway, before deciding to cut him loose. The sheriff agreed, believing that the real unsub was still out there, waiting to strike again.

TISHA WAS STILL grieving the loss of those poor gopher tortoises when she arrived at Glenn's house, parking in the driveway alongside his SUV. She hoped they would catch whoever was responsible. In the meantime, she welcomed an opportunity for a meal with a friendly and handsome face.

Wearing her hair down, she kept her attire simple with a blue smocked sundress and sandals. It took only one ring of the bell before the door opened.

"Hey. Right on time." Glenn grinned at her.

"Didn't want to be late," Tisha admitted. She blushed under the weight of his gaze, even while checking him out in his lime-green polo shirt, brown linen pants and black loafers.

"Come in," he said.

The moment she stepped inside the foyer, Tisha found

herself practically knocked over by an excited black Lab. "And who is this?" she asked, playing with the dog, who seemed friendly enough.

"That's Riley," Glenn told her. "I can see that's he's quickly warming up to you."

"Must be that he senses that I love dogs." Tisha laughed. "I have one of my own."

"Cool." He ordered Riley to give her some breathing room and the dog obeyed the command without missing a beat.

Tisha quickly scanned the handsomely furnished, spacious interior of the house and said, "Really nice place you have here, including the property I saw when driving up."

"Thanks." Glenn seemed to downplay it. "It's enough right now for me and Riley. But if there ever need to be any additions, I'm happy to go there."

She suspected that he was referring to having a wife and family. But there would need to be a lot of children to actually outgrow the residence. "Good to know," she uttered nevertheless. As the pleasing odor of food passed to her nostrils, she asked, "Can I help with anything?"

"Nope. Got it covered. Make yourself at home."

She smiled. "I will, thanks."

"By the way, do you prefer white or red wine?" he asked curiously.

"Red would be great."

"Red, it is." He touched her arm affectionately. "Dinner will be served shortly."

"Good, as I'm starving," Tisha confessed.

He grinned and walked toward the big kitchen.

As she started to wander around the great room, Tisha spotted the acoustic guitar leaning up against a midcentury modern armchair. She picked it up and asked light-heartedly, "Do you play the guitar? Or is this only meant to impress visitors?"

"Maybe a little of both." Glenn laughed while checking a pot on the stove. "Yes, I play it from time to time as a way to keep Riley entertained. You play?"

"A little, but I'm not very good, I'm afraid, and way out of practice." Tisha strummed the guitar a little with her fingers. "I'm more at home with the piano, learning to play as a child." She had only recently sold the baby grand piano she had during her marriage, as her current residence was too small to keep it.

"Any musical talents are great to have," he told her.

"Very true," she agreed, while hoping he would play the guitar while she was there. In the meantime, Riley came up to Tisha and she petted his back and chest, which he clearly enjoyed in both instances. She imagined that the dog would get along well with Jacky, who was in need of a friendly canine companion.

When she was told it was time to wash up for dinner, Tisha went to the bathroom downstairs, while hoping to get a tour of the rest of the house, including where Glenn slept—alone, she assumed.

GLENN MARVELED AT just how stunning Tisha was as she sat across from him in a welted-back side chair at the oak dining room table. Even better was seeing her hair down. He'd love to run his fingers through it sometime.

"This is incredible," she said, breaking into his thoughts, while eating his home-cooked meal consisting of corned beef, sweet-potato pasta and lemon-flavored brussels sprouts. Along with red wine.

He smiled. "Thanks."

"Where did you learn to cook?" She gave him a curious gaze.

"Picked up pretty much everything I know about cooking from my sister, Josette. She's a few years older and a chef at an upscale restaurant, living in Anchorage with her partner."

"Cool." Tisha smiled and lifted her wineglass. "I've always wanted to visit Alaska."

"Went there once," he told her, forking some pasta. "Amazing place." He liked the idea of returning there with Tisha, whom he was certain Josette would love. "Do you have any siblings?" he asked.

"Just me, myself and I," she quipped. "My parents wanted more children, but it never happened. Guess some things aren't meant to be."

Glenn detected in her tone the regret of missing out on having children with her late husband. Maybe there was still a family in her future. And his own, for that matter.

"So how was your day?" he asked between bites, if only to break the stiffness in the air.

"Not very good, I'm afraid." Tisha frowned as she held in her fork a brussels sprout. "Someone shot and killed two gopher tortoises in the Manikeke Crossing."

"Sorry to hear that." Glenn tasted his wine. "I take it the culprit or culprits are still on the loose?"

She nodded. "Cowards and creeps."

"I couldn't agree more." He could see just how serious she took things in her job as a game warden, making him appreciate her all the more as someone who also loved nature and maintaining a healthy environment for all living species. "Had my own share of disappointment today," he remarked.

Tisha tilted her head. "What happened?"

"Thought we had a solid lead on a suspect in the murder of Tris Lindberg. A drifter had been following her, in the name of hitting her up for money. Unfortunately, it didn't add up in terms of him being her killer. Which also excluded him, more or less, from being a legitimate suspect as the Shellview County Killer."

"That's too bad." Tisha dabbed a paper napkin to her mouth. "All you can do is keep the investigation going till the right answers surface, right?"

"Right." He grinned at her. "Having you over for dinner has been right by me, in and of itself."

She showed her teeth. "For me, too."

As if he wanted in on the action, Riley barked in agreement from where he was sitting in corner observing them, then stood and came up to Tisha for some added attention.

After dinner, Glenn gave her a tour of the house, including one of the upstairs guest bedrooms that he had converted into a home office with traditional furnishings—he knew his job often required him to bring his work home with him. He gauged Tisha's reaction as she saw the spacious primary bedroom with its large windows, modern storage furniture and king-size platform bed. He was particularly interested in how she viewed the bed, imagining being in it with her, making love.

"Hmm…" she murmured. "Nice."

He smiled at her, content to leave it at that, then they went back downstairs and he showed her the grounds. She seemed equally taken with them and he found himself imagining her living there, with two dogs roaming around the property for them to chase after, like a fun-loving, energetic couple.

When they returned to the house, Tisha lifted the guitar and asked sweetly, "Will you play something for me?"

Glenn grinned, taking it from her, and responded, "I'd be happy to." He began playing the first song that came to mind, which happened to be one of the first songs he learned to play and among his favorites—"Always on Your Side."

Tisha's eyes lit up. "I love that song."

"Me, too." He smiled and was glad when she began to sing the lyrics, causing him to join in.

Afterward, they laughed like schoolchildren from the impromptu duet and Tisha looked him in the eye and asked in a sexy tone of voice, "Would it be alright if I kissed you…?"

"I would love it if you kissed me," Glenn told her without prelude.

She cupped his cheeks and laid one on his lips. Her mouth was as soft as he imagined and a good fit for his. The kiss was just long enough to make his heart race, before she pulled away.

"Sorry about that." Tisha blushed flirtatiously. "I don't know what came over me."

Glenn laughed. "Whatever it was, you won't find me complaining."

"Good to know." She laughed back. "I think I should go now."

"Okay." He wanted her to stay but didn't want to put any pressure on her. When and if she was all in, he would be ready.

"Thanks for the dinner."

"Anytime," he told her and meant it. "I'll walk you out."

Moments later, Glenn watched her drive off, as did Riley, who already acted as though he had lost his best friend. "Don't worry, boy," he told the dog optimistically. "If we play our cards right, Tisha will be back, and we can pick up where we left off."

They went back inside the house with that thought very much on Glenn's mind.

Chapter Six

Tisha drove off feeling pretty good about spending some quality time away from work with a man. Or this one, in particular.

She had actually kissed him. Imagine that. And he was clearly receptive to it, but respectful enough to not want to go too far too soon.

But there was always the next time. Or one after that.

She glanced at the ring on her finger contemplatively. It had taken her a while to get past the tragedy of losing her husband at such a young age. Maybe now, there was an opportunity to move on and find happiness again with someone.

When she arrived home, Jacky greeted Tisha excitedly and she hugged the dog endearingly. She imagined Jacky would get along well with Riley and form her own bond.

After taking a shower, Tisha slipped into a cotton chemise and headed for her bedroom, which had two large windows, handcrafted log furniture and a queen-size panel bed. She hated sleeping alone and longed for someone to hold and be held by.

Glenn flooded her thoughts in the moment before sleep overtook her.

The following day, Tisha joined other game wardens,

Bree and Sherman, and their supervisor, Sergeant Fritz Alvarez, as they zeroed in on the culprits who had killed the two gopher tortoises. The three suspects were bloodthirsty teenagers who had been discovered from a video they took of the killing, which they posted on online sites, all but bragging about their cruel actions.

"How dumb can they be?" Fritz asked. His tall and muscular frame was rigid as he peered at the trio they had tracked to a recreational area along the Chattahoochee River, hanging out as though they didn't have a care in the world. "Who does something like that, then posts it online for everyone to see—including us—and still expects to get away with it, as if they'd done nothing wrong?"

Tisha frowned and answered with indignation, "Teens who are truly sick, undisciplined and could care less about what they've done."

"Not to mention some of the other bizarre postings they put up," Bree said, "indicating a complete lack of compassion for wildlife and no appreciation for conservation."

"I'll go one step further," Sherman said thickly. "These kids are unsupervised delinquents who will have to pay the price for their actions."

"That we can agree on," Fritz stated, jutting his chin. "Let's bring them in..."

They wasted no time surrounding the three suspects—two older teen males and one petite female, who Tisha imagined couldn't have been more than fourteen or fifteen years old. They all seemed unfazed by being discovered and the seriousness of their current predicament.

"You're under arrest for what you did to those gopher tortoises," Fritz snapped at them.

As they were being handcuffed, the three were defiant, spouting off obscenities and taunts. "Get it off your chest," Sherman said sarcastically. "It won't do anything to get you out of the mess you've created."

Tisha seriously doubted that the suspects even cared, making it even more sad. But at least the culprits had been captured, preventing them from killing other tortoises.

They were facing charges that included the killing of threatened species, along with felony cruelty to animals—each were third-degree felonies carrying a maximum penalty of a fine totaling 10,000 dollars and as many as five years behind bars.

As far as Tisha was concerned, it was a price that needed to be paid, with protecting such species a priority. She felt the same way about holding persons accountable for human loss, as in the case of Tris Lindberg.

THAT AFTERNOON, Glenn sat at his desk and requested a video chat with his former advisor when he was a student at Georgia Southern University, Edward Kundu, an associate professor of criminology in the College of Behavioral and Social Sciences. He also happened to be a renowned criminal profiler, having written several books, with a particular interest in serial homicides. It was in this capacity that Glenn hoped to gain some insight into the elusive Shellview County Killer he was currently pursuing.

Professor Kundu accepted the invitation and appeared on the screen. An Indian American, he was in his late fifties with short gray hair and had a full salt-and-pepper beard. He touched his low-bridge eyeglasses and said with a grin, "Hi, Glenn. Nice to speak to you again."

Smiling back and almost feeling as though he was still

an undergrad, Glenn responded formally, "You, too, Professor Kundu."

"Edward is fine," he reminded Glenn, as they'd become friends over the years.

"Okay." Glenn met his brown eyes fixedly. "Did you have a chance to look over the file on my serial killer investigation?"

"I did." Edward sat back in his own high-backed office chair musingly. "Well, my first thought in sizing up this Shellview County serial killer is that he's no more, no less a predator than those who have perpetrated serial murders before him. Jack the Ripper, Albert Fish, Ted Bundy, Henry Lucas, John Wayne Gacy, Gerald Gallego, Richard Ramirez, Charles Ng, Samuel Little—the list goes on. Or, in other words, there's nothing particularly special about this unsub. He's targeting people—mostly women—who have come into his crosshairs through one means or another. That being said, he's clearly chosen to strangle his victims rather than shoot, stab, hang, push off a cliff, or use some other dastardly means to kill—which, in and of itself, puts him in a certain category of serial killers. They gain some sort of perverse thrill in this mode of execution."

Glenn asked, "So apart from the murders themselves, what is the unsub gaining by killing the victims? Are we talking about doing this for sport, to see just how long he can get away with it, or what? Or is there a psychological angle here that might help me get a better fix on what we're dealing with?"

Edward touched his glasses while pondering the question, then said frankly, "There's always a psychological component to serial homicides. Most serial killers are

psychopaths by their very nature, which shouldn't be confused with being certifiably insane. Quite the opposite.
Few serial killers—virtually none—are so far gone so
as to not be able to distinguish between right and wrong,
or reality and fantasy or illusion. That notwithstanding,
mental illness to some degree is nearly always a corre-
late of serial killing, as normal triggers fail to get the
killer to stop after the first kill. Or even the second one."
Edward scratched his beard. "The psychological insta-
bility is often born out of conflicts the killer is coping
with internally—be it relationship, work, financial issues
or something else—that he or she deals with externally
by killing others to relieve the pressure. Only to have
that tension rebuild time and time again. Till the killer is
stopped through means other than a willingness to quit."

Glenn considered what had been laid out by the associate professor as if he was still a student. But now that
he was a seasoned GBI special agent, he could interpret
things differently, and said to him, "I get that the unsub
has psychological issues, while also being clever enough
to avoid detection. Are there any other characteristics,
physical or otherwise, to look for while I'm narrowing
the search for him?"

"As I'm sure you know, serial killers come in all
shapes, sizes and sexes, racial and ethnic backgrounds,
marital status, professions and net worth, et cetera," Edward pointed out and drew a breath. "But that doesn't
mean that serial killers aren't more prone to fall into
some categories than others—such as being mostly in
their midtwenties to midforties, being loners in their actions, if not lifestyles. They have some proclivity to commit or have learned violence through others whether when

young or older and have likely experienced some sort of familial dysfunction or childhood trauma that is a factor in the present antisocial behavior. That pretty much sums it up in terms of profiling your unsub. Whether that can make a difference in the investigation will be for you to decide. Either way, I'm always happy to be of assistance whenever I can, Glenn."

"I appreciate that," he told him, offering a nod. "And you have provided valuable insight to add to the profile of the unsub as the investigation continues and we try to nab him as soon as possible."

"Good." Edward leaned forward. "If you're unable to get the guy soon and want to try to get inside the head of a like-minded serial killer, you might consider talking to a man named Lucas Conseco. Five years ago, Conseco was convicted of strangling to death eight women in Fulton County. He's currently serving a life sentence at the Macon State Prison in Oglethorpe, Georgia."

"I'm familiar with the case," Glenn said as he pondered the matter. Lucas Conseco had murdered women named Linda or Lynda, as a warped act of revenge against his deceased mother, who had abused then abandoned him in childhood. The GBI had assisted the Fulton County Sheriff's Office and Atlanta Police Department in solving the strange case.

Edward said matter-of-factly, "I'm actually writing a book on Conseco and have interviewed him. I'd be happy to help set it up if you'd like to see what he has to say about the inner workings of a fellow serial strangler killer, if that might help your cause…"

"I don't think I need to go there," Glenn said, respectfully declining the suggestion. He winced at the thought of using one serial killer to capture another. "But I'll keep it in mind, nevertheless," he added, if only for effect.

"Alright."

Glenn ended the video chat and left the office to head down the hall and into the office of the special agent in charge, Rhianna Kingsley. She was leaning up against a black height-adjustable standing desk near a window wall, while looking at some papers, and noticed him enter.

"Hey," she said evenly. "What's going on?"

"Just spoke with a criminal profiler on the Shellview County Killer investigation," Glenn told her.

"Really?" Her eyes widened with curiosity.

He gave her a summary of the discussion and added, "Gives us something more to place into the equation in our efforts to home in on a suspect."

"Interesting." Rhianna nodded. "Whatever it takes to solve this case."

"That's how I'm working it," he stressed.

When their cell phones rang at the same time, Glenn suppressed a grin, as each responded to the calls. For him, it was Sheriff Marjorie Pierce on the line.

"There's been another murder," she told him bleakly.

"Where?" He regarded Rhianna, whose expression suggested she had received equally disturbing news.

"Kendell State Park," Marjorie replied flatly. "The death fits the pattern of the serial murders…"

"I'm on my way." Glenn disconnected and saw that Rhianna was already off the phone.

With a dour look on her face, she muttered, "Guess we received the same notification. The Shellview County Killer has apparently struck again."

Wishing he could push back against the notion, but

unable to, Glenn furrowed his brow and said forlornly, "Yeah, it appears that way..."

MARJORIE WAS ANGUISHED as she conferred with her deputies at the crime scene of Kendell State Park on Rawley Road, where the victim had been found in the woods, along a trail, lying flat on her back.

Identified as Patrina Morse, a thirty-three-year-old high school teacher who was visiting from Sydney, Australia, she was staying at the Kendell State Park Lodge and had gone out for a morning run, when disaster struck in the form of a killer.

Marjorie studied the deceased white woman, who was slender with short dark brown curly hair. She was wearing a yellow tank top, dark gray leggings and white sneakers. Gazing at her neck, Marjorie could see the discoloration on it, a telltale sign that she had been strangled. Much like the four other victims that had fallen prey to ligature strangulations, perpetrated by a serial killer. Similarly, there was the clear indication of puncture wounds that likely came from a stun gun, per the unsub's modus operandi.

The fact that this one happened so soon after the murder of Tris Lindberg was troubling to Marjorie, to say the least. Did this speak of desperation on the part of the unsub? Or sheer arrogance that he could handpick any target of his choosing and operate with little fear of apprehension?

Either way, she loathed that this was happening under her watch. Along with that of GBI Agent Glenn McElligott, who had to be just as ticked off with the case and its dynamics as she was. They would either sink or swim together on this one. She was determined that it would be the latter, as Marjorie watched the special agent working his way through the crime scene tape and as he approached her.

GLENN COULD SEE the strain on Sheriff Pierce's face as she greeted him at the spot where the body was found. Not that he could blame her for feeling the pressure, just as he was. And now they had a new victim to contend with.

"What are we looking at?" he asked her routinely, even if it was painfully obvious, as Glenn glanced at the pale and tragic homicide victim, and back to the sheriff.

Marjorie pursed her lips and replied tonelessly, "Name's Patrina Morse. Three days ago, Ms. Morse and a female friend, Tracy Nguyen, arrived from Australia for a vacation—staying at the Kendell State Park Lodge. According to Ms. Nguyen, at approximately nine a.m. today, Ms. Morse went out for a run. She was an avid jogger. When she didn't return by noon, Ms. Nguyen went looking for her…only to find her friend dead deep in the woods…"

"Did she happen to see anyone else before discovering the body?" Glenn asked the sheriff, wondering if the killer could have still been in the area.

"Apparently not." Majorie hunched her shoulders. "However, as she was under duress after calling 911 and afterward, which is totally understandable, we will need to question her further on that front."

"Good." Glenn frowned while thinking that he needed to speak to the witness himself and see what he could gather from her. "We'll need to access any surveillance cameras at the lodge or elsewhere in and around the park." He was thinking that the killer could have followed the victim from the lodge, unbeknownst to her, before killing her and disappearing into the woods.

"Trust me, my department will use every angle at our disposal to try and solve this murder," she told him.

"Of course." He didn't mean to step on her toes, if that was what the sheriff thought. They were all on the same page. Hell, the same book and chapter in trying to solve the murder. "Looks like our unsub is at it again."

"I know," Marjorie groaned. "I'm sure the medical examiner's office will back us up on this." She sighed. "Look at her. She didn't deserve that while on vacation in Georgia."

"Yeah."

Glenn gazed at the victim, imagining how this would hit her family in Australia. Being in the wrong state at the worst possible time was something her friend would have to live with for the rest of her life. But at least she would have a life to live.

Not so for Patrina Morse.

When Ned Karakawa, the associate medical examiner, and his team arrived, Glenn had already set the GBI crime scene investigators and those from the sheriff's department in motion in the collection of evidence, including photographs of the victim and surrounding area.

Karakawa wrinkled his brow as he glanced at Marjorie and then looked at Glenn and remarked humorlessly, "Wish we didn't have to keep meeting like this…"

"It does stink," Glenn muttered truthfully.

"Tell me about it," Marjorie concurred, as they stepped aside to allow him to conduct his preliminary examination of the body.

It didn't take long for Karakawa to indicate his belief

that they were looking at a victim of homicide by ligature strangulation.

Glenn filled in the rest himself, as it was fairly obvious to him that this was the work of the Shellview County Killer, who seemed more than happy to rub it in their faces.

TISHA WAS GIVEN a start with the news from Glenn that an Australian woman had been murdered in Shellview County and the case was linked to the serial killer. The fact that the heinous act had taken place at Kendell State Park was even more disturbing, as it fell within her work section. *How many more people have to die?* she asked herself grimly, as she arrived at the park. It was teeming with county and state law enforcement, along with bystanders, as if they had nothing better to do than watch a murder investigation unfold.

She saw Glenn speaking with Sherman and the sheriff, and joined them. "Came as soon as I heard," Tisha told them.

"Warden Fletcher," Marjorie said, acknowledging her.

"Sheriff." Tisha met her eyes, imagining just how much she was stressing out while overseeing this investigation. "How's it going?" she asked of the investigation.

"Apart from the cold-blooded murder of a tourist, about as well as could be expected with little to go on for the time being," the sheriff responded sourly.

Tisha turned to a frowning Sherman, who muttered, "Another murder happening within our jurisdiction is not good."

"No, it isn't," she acknowledged. "But given the wide range we cover, it's not too surprising, in and of itself."

Tisha twisted her lips. "The implication that it is again the work of a serial killer is another matter altogether." Differentiating those truths didn't make this go down any easier.

"True." He nodded thoughtfully and started talking to the sheriff.

Facing Glenn, Tisha said awkwardly, "Hey." The kiss they'd shared briefly yesterday crossed her mind.

"Hey." He met her gaze squarely. "Sorry about having to deal with the latest homicide."

"Me, too," she admitted. "Thanks for the heads-up, which came just before I received the news from my work section boss, Sergeant Fritz Alvarez."

"I wanted to keep you up to date on the twists and turns of this case," Glenn told her, "since you were pulled into it after the discovery of the last victim—"

Tisha winced. "So the MO in the latest murder is the same?" Not that she had any reason to believe the homicide was unrelated to the Shellview County Killer case.

"I'm afraid so." He tilted his head. "She was strangled with a ligature, with evidence that a stun gun was used on the victim."

Tisha made a face. "How horrifying."

"The autopsy will likely clear up any doubt," Glenn said. "But as it stands at the moment, the victim, Patrina Morse, was targeted by the serial killer, however she managed to fall into his crosshairs."

In that instant, they both looked to the right and watched uneasily as the decedent was being carted away by the associate medical examiner, whose work, to Tisha, would only add to the trauma inflicted upon the victim, even if they were unable to feel it on a human level.

HE WATCHED THE goings-on taking place at the Kendell State Park, keeping his distance but keenly aware that they were investigating the latest murder he had committed. Frankly, he was not too taken with the Shellview County Killer moniker the press had hoisted upon him like a badge of dishonor.

As far as he was concerned, it was totally honorable to end the lives of those whom he had sought out and extinguished like burning flames when their time had come to be snuffed out. He made no apologies for doing what needed to be done. For that matter, he had no qualms about going after others who were slated for death by his hands.

He studied the pretty game warden who was chatting amicably with the GBI special agent. Seemed as if they were more interested in one another than solving the murder of the good-looking Australian teacher he had strangled to death.

He imagined that the game warden would be easy prey, like the others, when the time was right. Maybe the GBI agent, too, if he got in his way. Much like when the IT manager who'd lost his life when he made the mistake of interfering with plans to kill the attractive girlfriend.

The Shellview County Killer remained hidden in plain view for a bit longer, relishing the attention he was getting and the ineffectiveness of the authorities to stop him. Then he quietly and calmly slipped away into the woods and farther out of reach from those who would wish to prevent him from killing again.

Chapter Seven

Kendell State Park Lodge was just miles from the Chattahoochee River and the park itself, steep in loblolly pine and red maple trees, with a waterfall and more than one trail. Glenn saw these as possible escape routes the killer of Patrina Morse had taken. He mused about this while approaching the cabin, alongside Tisha, whom he had invited to accompany him in his interview with the victim's friend and traveling companion, Tracy Nguyen.

Before they could knock, the door opened. A slim thirtysomething woman with shoulder-length brunette hair in a blunt cut stood there. Glenn met her brown eyes, reddened from crying, and asked to be sure, "Are you Tracy Nguyen?"

She nodded. "Yes."

He flashed his identification. "GBI Special Agent McElligott and this is Game Warden Fletcher. We need to ask you a few questions about Patrina Morse, as part of the investigation into her death."

Her voice shook as she responded with an accent, "Okay."

Rather than invite them inside the cabin that Glenn could see through the opening had the standard modern furnishings and some luggage, Tracy stepped out onto the porch, closing the door. With the space between cabins and relative privacy, this was fine by him as a place to talk.

He eyed Tisha then favored Tracy with an even look. He began, "I'd like to go over what you told Sheriff Pierce as to the timeline of your arrival at the lodge, up to the moment when you located Ms. Morse."

"I'm still just processing everything that happened," she cautioned, "but I'll try…"

"You're from Sydney, Australia?" he asked.

"Yes, we both lived there and taught at Blanden High School."

Tisha spoke in a friendly tone. "Long ways from home."

"It was actually my idea to travel to the States," Tracy explained, "having visited once before as a child."

"What made you choose Georgia this time around?" Glenn queried.

"Seemed like a nice place when searching online for possible states to visit. As we both love the outdoors, Kendell State Park checked all the boxes…" Her voice dropped. "Never imagined anything like this could happen—"

"I know," Tisha said sympathetically, touching her hand. "If you need a moment…"

"I'm fine." Tracy wiped tears from her eyes and looked at Glenn. "What else would you like to know?"

"Since you've been at the park, has anyone ever approached either Ms. Morse or you that was threatening in any way?" he asked her.

"Not that I can recall," she stated.

"What about nonthreatening?" Tisha regarded her.

"Maybe someone you met on one of the trails. Or perhaps at the lodge's restaurant or bar?"

Tracy mulled this over for a long moment, then said, "Come to think of it, there was one man we met while sightseeing the day we arrived. He didn't really hit on us or anything, but did seem interested in the fact that we were Aussies. We talked a bit and that was pretty much it."

Or maybe there was more to this man, Glenn thought. "Can you describe him?"

"Thirties, white, dark-haired, tall and in good shape. Not bad on the eyes. Definitely American." Her brow furrowed. "Do you think he could have killed Patrina?"

"Probably not, but we need to look into every possibility," Glenn told her somewhat reassuringly. As it was, the description was, at the very least, consistent with an unidentified suspect seen on surveillance video related to the serial killer investigation. Could this be their perpetrator? "To that effect, I'd like to send over a sketch artist to speak with you, if that would be okay."

"That's fine." She wiped her nose with the back of her hand. "But just so you know, I'll be going home as soon as the sheriff gives me permission to bring Patrina back to Sydney for a proper burial."

"I understand." He nodded sympathetically, knowing they would need a day or two to complete the autopsy and any additional gathering of forensic evidence from the victim.

Tisha gazed at her and asked curiously, "With a number of trails in Kendell State Park, what made you go look for your friend on that trail, in particular?"

"We'd been on that trail every day since we've been here," Tracy said straightforwardly. "It seemed the likely route Patrina would take for her run." She sighed. "If only she had taken a different route—"

"She had no way of knowing she was running into danger," Glenn said, aware that this was little consolation for the death of her friend and colleague, very likely caused by a serial killer.

"That's the truly sad part to have to deal with." Tracy sniffled and Tisha put an arm around her to comfort her. "You will catch whoever did this, won't you?"

"We will," Tisha promised.

Glenn doubled down on this as he said firmly, "We'll do whatever it takes to bring Ms. Morse the justice she deserves."

After they had left the lodge, Glenn was behind the wheel of his Dodge Durango Pursuit, with Tisha in the passenger seat. "So what's your take on the latest homicide?" he asked her.

She waited a beat and answered, "For starters, my guess is that Patrina Morse's killer followed her to the Blakely Trail, which is one of the most popular trails at Kendell State Park, but with enough twists, turns and obscured sections to hide a predator...and probably caught her off guard when he attacked her."

"I was thinking the same thing," he said. "Whether the unsub was the same person they met as sightseers remains to be seen, but it's definitely worth checking out."

"True." Tisha gazed at him. "There should be video surveillance in enough places around the park to maybe narrow down some suspects."

"And possibly other witnesses, as well, who may have seen someone come or go that corresponds to the timeline in which the murder took place."

She drew a breath. "With all of the murders occurring within the Georgia Department of Natural Resources Region 5 Law Enforcement Division—two of which have taken place in my work sections—it leaves me wondering if there is a pattern in there somewhere that needs to be explored."

Glenn lifted an eyebrow as he glanced at her and back to the road. "You think the perp could be someone within your ranks?"

"Not necessarily," she said swiftly, "as I'd hate to go there without any rock-solid proof, but possibly someone who knows the region well and is comfortable moving around the area while being inconspicuous at the same time."

"Hmm..." he uttered contemplatively. "Makes sense. I'll pass that thought on to Sheriff Pierce and we'll look into it as part of the broader investigation."

"Okay." She paused. "I feel so sorry for Tracy. Having to end her vacation so tragically like that—"

"I know." He reached across and touched Tisha's hand. It was soft and fit into his like it was meant to be there. "The unsub won't get away with this," he promised and thought, *or any of his other killings*.

She squeezed his fingers but didn't say anything. Nor did she pull her hand away.

When he parked next to Tisha's truck, Glenn felt like this was a moment in which a display of affection was warranted. At least it felt right to him. He met her eyes squarely and said hotly, "My turn to kiss you. Are you game?"

Holding his gaze, Tisha uttered, "Yes, I'm game. Go for it!"

He did, lifting her chin and putting their mouths together. He slightly opened his, for a short kiss that became a long one. Both had to catch their breaths when he pulled away and said to her coolly, "See you later."

She touched his mouth with her fingers, smiled prettily and told him cheerfully, "Hope so. 'Bye."

With that, Tisha left his SUV and Glenn waited until she was inside her truck and headed out, before he followed briefly, his thoughts meandering between the sparks that kissing her had ignited in him like a slow-burning flame, and yet another woman being strangled by a relentless killer.

TISHA SPENT THE rest of the afternoon doing her rounds, covering more ground than usual in looking for any signs of trouble. Fortunately, she didn't find anyone suspicious lurking about to have to deal with. She touched her lips for seemingly the umpteenth time, where Glenn had kissed her, and she had kissed him back with equal ardor. There was clearly something delightful happening between them that she fully embraced, wanting nothing more than to see it through. And Tisha prayed that she might finally have a shot at happiness again that she feared might elude her forever.

But in the meantime, staying grounded was a smart thing. That included realizing that she would be competing for Glenn's time with a homicide investigation that managed to touch them both on different levels and needed to be solved for Shellview County, the victims and whatever the future may hold for her and the GBI special agent.

When she got home that day, after dropping by a fast-food restaurant for a fruit salad and coffee, Tisha put on Jacky's leash and took the dog out for a walk and to do her business. She couldn't wait for her to meet Riley and vice versa. Getting their dogs close would be a good thing in building a relationship between her and Glenn.

That night, Tisha brushed and flossed her teeth, showered and went to bed, thinking about Glenn and what they might do beneath her cotton sateen sheets. She drifted off as her thoughts turned to the ongoing serial killer investigation and the latest victim's devastating turn of events while on vacation from Australia.

GLENN STOOD AT the billiard table inside Becklyn's Bar on Flat Rock Road in Midland. On the other side was GBI Special Agent Kurt Stewart. Both were holding pool cues while they played. A nearby table held a half-filled pitcher of beer, along with their mugs. Glenn was glad to have a colleague to bounce his thoughts off regarding the current case he was assigned to, where, in all likelihood, there were now five homicide victims, with apparently a single perpetrator.

"This guy is proving to be a handful," Glenn muttered, as he lined up the cue and calmly drove a ball into the corner pocket. "I wouldn't go so far to say that he's toying with us, but the unsub has managed to spread his homicidal tendencies across Shellview County, with no signs of letting up. At least not till we can bring him in."

"He's not invincible!" Kurt asserted, creasing his brow while leaning against the table. "Far from it. The way I see things, the unsub has simply gotten the dice to roll in his favor, thus far. Not because he's some kind of genius or anything, but more that, like other serial killers he's taken advantage of the loopholes in society that can give some murderers just enough room to maneuver in killing, without getting caught. Till that happens…and eventually it will."

"I agree," Glenn said succinctly, and missed the next shot as he lost his concentration. If he hadn't known better, he would think that this had been Kurt's intention all along, to distract him just enough to lose the game. But he felt otherwise, as everything the special agent said made perfect sense. "Unfortunately, the longer this thing goes on, the more concerned I am that the unsub will take his act elsewhere, before we can slap the cuffs on, lock him up and toss the key into the river."

"That's not likely to happen." Kurt set his jaw and studied the table. "The perp is obviously someone who's at home with the outdoors and seems to know the lay of the land, making him overconfident. This will be to his detriment eventually." He drove a ball into a side pocket. "Until then, he's staying put, where he's comfortable sizing up his prey and taking action to that effect."

Glenn chuckled and tasted his beer. "Maybe we should trade places and you can take over this investigation," he quipped.

Kurt laughed. "Would if I could. As it is, the GBI's Commercial Gambling Unit would never let me go, as long as the investigation is in full steam and yielding results."

"I understand. It was worth a try," Glenn said lightheartedly. In truth, he would never turn over a case to someone else because of an inability to solve it himself. That would mean failure. Something that wasn't in his vocabulary. Or DNA.

"Doesn't mean I can't pitch in on my own time," Kurt offered. "Whatever I can do to help, just let me know."

"Will do." Glenn watched as his friend missed a shot, putting him back in control. "For now, I think that working with the Shellview County Sheriff's Department, and the DNR's Law Enforcement Division to a lesser degree, should be enough to solve this case—presumably sooner than later."

"Cool." Kurt grabbed his mug of beer and tasted. "And how are things going with your mystery woman?"

Glenn laughed. "Wouldn't exactly call her a mystery woman. Enchanting would be more like it," he admitted, recalling the effect her kisses had on him. "In fact, she's a game warden and, in answer to your question, it's still a work in progress."

"Well, just don't work too hard, McElligott," he said with a chuckle. "At least not till you see if your game warden can put the hex on you."

I think she already has, Glenn told himself truthfully, but responded contemplatively, "I'll try to remember that."

In the meantime, he called the winning shot in a corner pocket and drilled it.

Half an hour later, Glenn was at home, where he playfully wrestled with Riley for a bit and then headed up to his office and laptop to study what he knew thus far on the Shellview County Killer and where he needed to go from here.

On Wednesday afternoon, Tisha put on a light blue crop top and matching leggings with her exercise sneakers and went to the Blair Bay Fitness Center, joining her friend Jeanne for a Zumba workout.

As the group class was warming up, Tisha blurted out what she had to tell someone, if only to share her excitement, "So I've met someone—"

"Oh, really?" Jeanne batted her eyelashes curiously. "Do tell?"

"He's a GBI special agent," Tisha told her thoughtfully.

"How nice." She grinned in approval.

"Glenn also happens to be the lead investigator in the Shellview County Killer case," Tisha pointed out.

Jeanne faced her. "Does that include the Aussie who was killed yesterday at Kendell State Park?"

Tisha nodded. "Afraid so."

Jeanne frowned. "How terrible for her."

"Right?" Tisha concurred and did some stretches. "Never should have happened."

"But it did. Just like the others. When will it end?"

"Wish I could answer that," Tisha responded truthfully. "I suppose it'll end when the authorities get the break they need to crack the case."

"I suppose." Jeanne drew a breath. "Anyway, it's about time you put yourself out there again."

"I was thinking the same thing." Tisha relished the thought, even if it made her a little nervous as well. She felt vulnerable to some extent in getting back into the dating game. But it needed to happen. Wherever things between her and Glenn ended up.

"Hope this works out for you, Tisha."

"Me, too."

She smiled with her teeth, and then wondered when Jeanne might also be ready to get back to meeting people now that her divorce was in the rearview mirror. Or had the bad blood between her and her ex soured her on romance for the foreseeable future?

As they began to get into the Zumba dance workout, Tisha thought about taking that next step with Glenn and what that might mean when there was no turning back. It was something she felt ready for. But was he?

Chapter Eight

On Saturday, Tisha got up the nerve to invite Glenn over for lunch. Actually, it was less about courage and more about the anticipation of seeing him again and in her own comfort zone. He didn't strike her as being the type of man who needed a comfort zone of his own, per se, when it came to socializing.

When his phone rang, her heart skipped a beat as if she had second thoughts. But she did not. She was going for it, no matter the result.

"Hey," he said amicably when answering.

"Hey." She took a moment, then said, "I was wondering if you'd like to have lunch with me today, at my house?"

"Absolutely." His voice lifted a notch. "Count me in."

"I will." Tisha chuckled while flipping her ponytail across one shoulder. "And feel free to bring Riley along. Jacky could use the company."

"Consider it done. Riley would love to develop a camaraderie with Jacky."

"Then it's a date," she spoke cheerfully. Wasn't it? "How does one o'clock work for you?"

"Like a charm," he said smoothly. "We'll be there."

"Wonderful." Tisha texted him her address. "See you in a couple of hours."

"Count on it!"

After disconnecting, Tisha tried to temper her enthu-siasm as she put on a lilac knit shirt and skinny ankle jeans, and went barefoot while tidying the town house. Not that it needed much cleaning, as she was somewhat of a neat freak and Jacky was house-trained and otherwise not prone to making a mess of things. Still, after having seen Glenn's house, where seemingly nothing was out of order, Tisha felt the pressure to make him feel just as comfortable as she had felt when visiting him.

For lunch, she made marinated vegetable salad and turkey frittata, to go with peach lemonade. *Hope he likes this*, Tisha told herself in the kitchen, after admittedly being out of practice in cooking for two. Not to mention trying to measure up to Glenn's cooking, having a chef sister to learn from.

Chill, Tisha mused, realizing that they weren't in com-petition. Besides, she didn't necessarily agree that the key to a man's heart was his stomach. She sensed that it took more than that to win Glenn over. Was that what she was trying to do? Or was it more a desire to win each other over to see what they could both bring to the table in a potential relationship?

As she stood over the countertop, Tisha stared at the wedding ring on her finger for a moment, then removed it. She headed upstairs and put the ring in a drawer. It was time, she knew, and she wanted to embrace whatever may lie ahead with a clean slate.

When Jacky started barking, Tisha realized that com-pany had arrived. "You must feel the positive vibes of making a new friend, don't you, girl?" she asked the dog with a chuckle, following her downstairs. Tisha slipped into some slingback flats, went to the door and opened it.

"Hey," Glenn said on the other side. He was sporting a big grin and looking great in a red button-up shirt, jeans and brown Chelsea boots. Next to him was Riley, his tail wagging with eagerness to go inside.

"Hey." Tisha smiled. "Come in, both of you." The moment they did, the dogs quickly sized each other up. "Riley, this is Jacky. Jacky, Riley." As they seemed to grow comfortable with one another, Tisha told Glenn, "Jacky is a retired K-9 with the DNR Law Enforcement Division. She still has game, but has happily left her old life behind."

"Good for her," Glenn remarked as he walked up to the dog and began to play with her naturally. He said to Jacky, in a smooth voice, "Nice to hear that you were one of us."

Jacky seemed more than amenable, easily warming up to him and the attention. As if not wanting to be left out of the loop, Riley joined in on the action. Glenn had no problem playing with both dogs for a moment, before Tisha came to his rescue and let them both out in the back-yard to get to know each other better.

"Looks as if they've already become best buds," Glenn said with a laugh.

"I agree." Tisha chuckled and thought that was a good sign all the way around. "Hope you're hungry?"

"I am." He met her eyes and she nearly melted while interpreting his thoughts on the carnal side of hunger. She felt this sexual craving, too. "I like your place, by the way," he said, seemingly intent on breaking away from the moment.

"Thank you." Tisha colored. "Lunch is ready. I'll set the table, and you can wash up in the kitchen, if you like."

"Okay." He gave her a crooked grin and walked to the stainless-steel sink.

A few minutes later, they were seated at the dining room table. Tisha waited with bated breath as Glenn dug into the turkey frittata, then declared, "It's delicious."

"Glad you approve," she told him, breathing a sigh of relief.

"How could I not?" He gazed at her from across the table. "You're gorgeous."

"I was talking about the food." Tisha giggled. "But I'll take the compliment, anyway."

"Just telling it as I see it—or you." Glenn forked some vegetable salad. "The fact that you clearly know your way around a kitchen is only a bonus, as far as I'm concerned."

She laughed. "Ditto."

He laughed, too, then said, "Guess that makes us a match."

"Oh, you think so, do you?" she teased him, while holding her glass of peach lemonade.

"Only one way to find out," he challenged her, a catch in his tone of voice.

Tisha swallowed some salad with expectation. "What exactly did you have in mind?"

Glenn got to his feet and pulled her up, close to his body. "How about this, for starters..." He planted a mouth-watering kiss on her lips, causing Tisha's knees to buckle, and unlocked their mouths just as she was really getting into it. "There's a lot more where that came from," he murmured.

"I hope so," she gushed, touching her swollen mouth.

He stared into her eyes. "I want to make love to you, Tisha."

"I want that, too." She could no longer deny her needs as a woman. Not with him. But there was still the practical side to be considered. Unplanned pregnancy. She wasn't on the pill. "What about protection?"

Glenn pulled out a condom packet from his pants. "Thought I'd bring one along, just in case—to be on the safe side."

Tisha smiled. "Looks like you've thought of everything."

"Honestly, I've only been able to think about one thing—pushing aside my current investigation that can wait for the time being—and that's you, simply put."

"Ohh…" Her lashes fluttered with the flattery. "That's sweet." She looked up at him happily. "I think I can say the same thing about you."

He kissed her again. "Good minds think alike."

Tisha felt a surge of desire well within as she took his hand and said teasingly, "Why don't we take this up to my bedroom and whatever happens, happens…"

An eager grin played on Glenn's lips as he responded soulfully, "That sounds like a plan to me."

Me, too, Tisha thought, excited about the prospect of making love to him and whatever might come after that.

IT WASN'T LOST on Glenn that Tisha had removed her wedding ring. This told him that she was, in fact, ready to give another man a try—both in bed and in a relationship. This thrilled him, as he, too, had reached the point in his life where he wanted romance and embraced the process that started with chemistry and kisses...and had led to Tisha's primary suite.

He glanced around the room, taking in the log furniture and panel bed in particular, before he centered his gaze on Tisha. She was removing her clothes and silently beckoning him to do the same, as if to make sure they bared their souls together.

In a hurry to comply, Glenn started to unbutton his shirt while kicking off his boots at the same time. He watched, turned on, as Tisha let down her hair and quickly removed her shirt, then her bra, revealing small but full breasts, and slid the skinny jeans down and across her narrow hips and shapely legs. Then came her panties, and she stood before him in the nude.

He caught up to her, now naked, too, while tossing the condom packet on the duvet cover, and marveled at her beauty from head to toe, even as Tisha asked tentatively, "You like?"

Glenn took a breath, as if that went without saying, but said, anyway, "I definitely like!"

She showed her teeth, giving him a once-over. "I like you, too," she murmured.

He cupped her cheeks and they kissed passionately, bodies pressed together, for a long and exhilarating moment, before Glenn lifted Tisha and carried her to the bed, then climbed in next to her. He tore open the packet and slipped on the protection in one fell swoop, before moving up to her, and they resumed tasting each other's mouths.

Though he had already worked himself up to a fevered pitch, Glenn preferred to show some restraint and go the foreplay route so that this first time could be slow and rewarding. He wanted to pleasure Tisha in a way that she had no regrets whatsoever in taking this next all-important step, as he was sure that regrets in their lovemaking could never be the case with him.

He used his hands and mouth to stimulate her wherever she wanted. Tisha's reaction to his touch, along with her breaths and moans, told him when he was getting it right. So he continued to satisfy her, loving every minute. Finally, she pulled him half atop her and uttered in a yearning tone of voice, "I'm ready to have sex with you—now!"

"As you wish," Glenn said to her hungrily, not needing to be told twice.

He moved onto her the rest of the way and was inside Tisha, and they made love like it was theirs for the taking. Neither backed off an inch as their mouths and bodies, in sync and perpetual motion, worked up a sweat. Glenn fought back the urge to release his needs until Tisha experienced the high first.

As if on the same wavelength, she arched her body toward his and cried out as she had her orgasm. Only then did he let go and soon joined her, quivering from the climax. They went at it hard, riding the rapids together for one final burst of ecstasy, before things settled down and they regained their equilibrium.

Rolling off to the side, Glenn caught his breath and asked curiously, "Was it everything you hoped it would be?"

"Yes!" she said, her voice rising emphatically. "And much more, actually. How about you?"

"I enjoyed every second," he declared, as if he could ever have felt otherwise. "You were amazing. You *are* amazing," Glenn added, correcting himself.

"Good to know." Tisha laughed. "You weren't so bad yourself."

He chuckled. "Happy to be of service." *And hopefully it won't be for the last time*, he thought.

"Likewise," she promised, draping a smooth lean leg across his. "Afternoon delight can be so much fun."

Tisha giggled and Glenn admitted, "I'll say. Nights and mornings could be fun, too."

"You think?"

"Absolutely." He kissed her shoulder while assessing how she felt about the prospect of keeping this going.

"I believe they could be at that," she told him with a lilt to her voice.

Glenn almost wished he had brought along a second condom, but he hadn't wanted to get ahead of himself. Just in case his instincts for the lunch invite and where things seemed to be headed between them had been wrong.

He would settle for another kiss for the time being and went for it. Tisha reciprocated and it gave Glenn reason to believe this really could be the start of something spectacular, beyond just sex. Great as it was, he was ready to have a real relationship with a person he was connecting with.

The momentum came to a halt as they heard the dogs barking, as though getting antsy in the backyard.

Tisha laughed. "Looks like Jacky and Riley want some of our attention to go their way."

Glenn laughed, too. "Yeah, guess they have a problem with being ignored."

"We'll have to do something about that."

He reluctantly agreed, knowing there would be more than enough other opportunities to pick up where they left off.

After getting dressed and letting Riley and Jacky back into the house, Tisha's cell phone rang. Glenn watched as she answered it. From the sound of things, the call pertained to her work. It reminded him that they both had active careers in branches of law enforcement that would be part of the equation were they to build a relationship. The fact that it gave them common ground they could both relate to was big in his mind and a positive sign for the future.

Glenn saw worry lines appear on Tisha's forehead as she said to the caller, "I'm on my way…"

"What's going on?" he asked when she disconnected.

"A little girl has gone missing," Tisha said, fear in her tone.

"Where?"

"Kendell State Park."

Without her needing to say anything more, Glenn knew it was the same park where Patrina Morse had been murdered. According to the autopsy report, her death had been ruled a homicide, and the cause was ligature strangulation. The serial killer was still at large.

It didn't take much for Glenn to assume Tisha was drawing the conclusion that the missing girl might also have been targeted by the Shellview County Killer. Though the MO didn't fit, Glenn wasn't in a position to rule anything in or out.

Not until the girl was found—hopefully, alive.

"I'm coming with you," Glenn told Tisha, wanting to do whatever he could to bring the girl home safe and sound. Beyond that, the investigation fell into his jurisdiction as well, all things considered.

"Okay," she said succinctly, her expression illustrating

her unease at their cases overlapping and the real possibility of a bad outcome for the missing girl.

Glenn found himself just as unnerved on that front.

Chapter Nine

Tisha was beside herself with concern as she sped toward Kendell State Park, having quickly changed from leisure clothing into her uniform. Glenn sat in the passenger seat, wearing the same clothes he had worn to her house. They had briefly entertained bringing their dogs along to assist in the search for the missing nine-year-old girl named Rosa Bachiller, but thought better of it, believing they would only be in the way. And possibly even hinder the efforts to find the girl.

As it was, the DNR's Law Enforcement Division had already dispatched its K-9 unit to assist in the effort, along with a Special Operations Group proficient in search-and-rescue missions. The sheriff's department was using drones to aid in the search of the park and its perimeter.

Not to be left out of the mix, Glenn had requested that the GBI Investigative Division's Child Abduction Response Team join in the all-hands-on-deck effort to locate the missing child and reunite her with her family.

But Tisha feared that even these moves might not be enough—every second the girl remained missing lessened her chances of survival. Particularly in light of the recent murder of Patrina Morse at the same location.

"We'll find her, won't we?" Tisha glanced at Glenn

worriedly. She sensed that they were on the same page insofar as drawing inferences between the two cases.

"Yes, we will," he insisted. "It's only been a couple of hours since she went missing. Without knowing all the details, chances are the girl got lost somehow. In a park that size with lots of places to go or hide, nooks and crannies, and twists and turns, it wouldn't be difficult to lose one's way, or get confused. We have to believe that's the most likely scenario—and not one where she's been abducted or murdered by someone..."

Tisha nodded, while reading between the lines. Though the *someone* Glenn spoke of could well be a serial killer looking for more victims in a familiar location, she didn't dismiss the possibility that the girl could have run into a child sexual predator on the prowl. Or another opportunist who may have taken her. How many children went missing each year in the country, only to never be seen or heard from again?

I can't allow myself to think of the worst-case scenario prematurely, Tisha told herself as she drove into the park. Glenn was right. Odds were that this would all end on a good note. Until proven to the contrary.

When Glenn's hand brushed against hers, Tisha couldn't help but recall the hot sex they had engaged in earlier, making her blush. He had been everything she could have imagined in bed. And then some. He seemed to feel the same way about her. Maybe she really had turned the corner and could make this work.

The musings were put on hold as Tisha's thoughts returned to the moment at hand, as they reached their destination and joined the others, including Sherman Galecki and Bree McDaniels.

Sherman regarded Tisha and said, "I imagine you're thinking the girl's disappearance might be related to the woman who was murdered in the park?"

"Hard not to consider the possibility," she admitted, though she was trying hard to stay positive.

"Doesn't seem to fit," he argued.

"I agree," Glenn said. "But not everything fits the way it's supposed to."

Bree said, "Based on what I know about kids that age, she probably got bored and wandered off somewhere and then, before she knew it, couldn't find her way back."

"If that's so," Tisha said, "it shouldn't be too difficult to track her down."

"That's the plan," Bree told her.

Sheriff Pierce, who had set up a command post near the area where the girl had vanished, apparently wandering away from a family get-together, said equably, "We've got searchers from multiple law enforcement agencies and volunteers combing every inch of the park, the river and beyond," Marjorie stressed, "We won't stop till we find Rosa Bachiller."

Tisha took that to heart as she and Glenn spoke to the parents, Bert and Eloise Bachiller, who claimed they had only taken their eyes off Rosa for a second, before she was gone. Other families told the same story of seeing her one moment and not the next.

Now, the clock was ticking to bring the missing girl back to them.

Joining in on the search after talking with the CART, Tisha led Glenn through the woods, while trying to put herself in the head of a nine-year-old girl, in the event that she had gone off on her own. With no predator involved. Which direction would she choose? Farther into the wooded area? Or toward the river?

I'll bet she headed for the river, Tisha told herself, knowing that there was less rugged terrain there and brush that she could come upon and maybe cross without actually going into the water. At which point, she would still be in the woods, but far enough away from the original point of disappearing that it would be harder for the K-9 unit to track. Much less, other law enforcement, including drones that might not pick her up above the dense trees.

"Could *he* have taken her in broad daylight?" a wide-eyed Tisha asked Glenn, certain he understood that she was referring to the so-called Shellview County Killer.

"Anything's possible," he admitted as they worked their way through the trees. "If so, they would likely still be in the park somewhere. As I understand it, the moment the girl was reported missing—within minutes of her disappearance—action was taken right away to block the exits and begin the search. Seems doubtful that our unsub would risk this type of exposure, given his MO." Glenn took a breath. "If anyone has Rosa, the kidnapper won't get very far—"

Just as Tisha pondered his words, they heard some shuffling ahead, behind a cluster of loblolly pine trees. Instinctively, she went for the Glock pistol she carried in her waistband holster. If they were to encounter danger, she would do whatever was necessary to defend herself and Glenn, who did not have his own firearm with him.

"Come out with your hands raised!" Tisha demanded.

"She means business," Glenn barked toughly. "And so do I."

At first, Tisha was unsure if anyone would appear. Or,

for that matter, if they were even dealing with a human. The forested park was home to all kinds of wildlife, including white-tailed deer, raccoons, rabbits and even black bears. Could one of these be the culprit?

Before they could consider their next move, Tisha saw a frightened girl emerge from behind the trees. She was small, with big brown eyes and short brown hair, and was wearing a red T-shirt, blue shorts and white sneakers. The clothing corresponded with what the missing girl was wearing.

"Are you Rosa Bachiller?" Tisha asked, handing Glenn her gun just in case an abductor was hiding and waiting for them to let down their guard.

She nodded. "Yeah."

"I'm Warden Fletcher and this is Agent McElligott." Tisha eyed her. "Are you okay?"

Rosa nodded again, jutting her chin. "Am I in trouble?"

"No." Glenn, who had tucked the gun in his waistband, took the liberty of responding in a soft voice. "We've been looking for you. Your parents were worried that something bad might have happened..."

"I just went for a walk," the girl explained. "And didn't realize I'd gone so far. I couldn't remember how to get back..." She rubbed her nose. "I just sat down behind the tree and waited. I knew someone would find me. Didn't mean to cause a fuss."

"We're just happy to see you safe and sound." Tisha flashed her teeth, elated to see that the girl appeared to be in good shape and unharmed.

"I'm fine," Rosa insisted and suddenly ran into Tisha's arms. "Thank you for coming."

Tisha hugged the girl, imagining someday having a

daughter of her own to dote over. She regarded Glenn, who grinned at her and breathed a sigh of relief as he got out his cell phone and announced that Rosa Bachiller had been located.

ON MONDAY, Glenn paid a visit to the Western Lab's Forensic Biology section of the GBI Division of Forensic Sciences, which happened to be located in the same building where he worked. He hoped that there might be some new scientific data relevant to the latest homicide he was working on, tying it, as well, to the overall serial killer investigation.

Layla Ramaswamy, a Crime Laboratory scientist, met him at her workstation. The thirtysomething analyst, who was thin with short black hair and wore oval eyeglasses and a white lab coat, smiled and said, "Good morning, Agent McElligott."

"Morning." He glanced at her monitor and lab table, then asked, "So what do you have for me?"

Layla touched her glasses and responded, "Well, we were able to collect DNA and fingerprints from the latest victim, Patrina Morse, as well as debris found at the crime scene. Putting aside those belonging to Ms. Morse, the DNA samples were sent to CODIS and compared with known and unknown forensic profiles. Unfortunately, we weren't able to get any hits. Sorry."

So was he, though Glenn had feared this might be the case. The unsub had made it difficult for anyone to tie him to the crimes through forensic evidence. "And the prints?"

"There were a few latent prints examined. They were put into the state's Automated Fingerprint Identification System for a possible match." She sighed. "Negative. We tried the FBI's Next Generation Identification system. Same result. Could be the prints had nothing to do with the murder."

"Perhaps," Glenn said musingly, allowing that they may have come from other runners or park visitors. But he didn't discount that the unsub simply wasn't in the databases. Not yet. "What about trace evidence?"

Layla's brown eyes lit up. "I did find something there…" she hinted. "The crime scene investigators collected fibers that proved to be a match for ones the medical examiner's office pulled from Ms. Morse's neck during the autopsy. The fibers are consistent with those in a cotton cord."

"The same type of cord used to strangle the other victims," Glenn said, thinking out loud.

"Yes," she confirmed sourly. "Based on comparison, there's every reason to believe that Ms. Morse was strangled to death by either the actual cotton cord, or the same roll that led to the deaths of those murdered by the Shellview County Killer—"

Glenn had already come to the same reluctant but undeniable conclusion. Still to be determined was the identity of the unsub. And, sadly, there was a very real likelihood that he was already targeting his next victim.

That afternoon, Glenn met with Tisha for lunch at Ivanka's Food Truck on Vixon Street in downtown Blair Bay, as they both broke away from their respective duties. In fact, since becoming intimate, they had been spending more time together, getting to know one another better. He liked this part of developing a relationship and was excited to see how far it went.

As they stood beneath crape myrtle blossoms, eating chili dogs, he gave her the rundown on the latest in his investigation into the serial killer. "Same rope was used to kill Patrina Morse," he said, finishing matter-of-factly, while using a napkin to wipe chili off his chin. "Not that there was much doubt as to who strangled her to death."

"I know." Tisha frowned. "If only stopping him from killing innocent people was as predictable," she muttered.

"We'll get there," Glenn vowed, in spite of the appearance that the battle to bring the unsub in to face justice was already lost. "The sheriff is just as determined to solve this, believe me."

"I do." Tisha bit into her chili dog. "The DNR is with you every step of the way—no matter the frustration of having some of the murders occur within our work sections."

Glenn regarded her. He thought about their locating Rosa Bachiller, unharmed, in Kendell State Park, thanks in large part to Tisha's instincts and knowledge of the landscape. "How's Rosa doing, anyway, now that she's been reunited with her parents?"

"She's good." Tisha put a smile on her face. "From what I understand, all's well that ended well for all concerned."

"Great to hear." Glenn grinned at her. "You can pat yourself on the back for that one. Who knows what might have happened had she been out there all day and night."

"I was only doing my job," Tisha said, downplaying it, while dabbing a napkin to one corner of her mouth. "And maybe turning back the clock to when I pulled a similar stunt as a girl...but managed to find my way back to my parents, who scolded me and hugged me endearingly at the same time."

"Good for them." He gazed at her and said thoughtfully, "I hope to meet your folks sometime."

"I'd like that," She met his eyes. "Same here—meeting your mom, stepdad, father and sister…"

"You will," he promised, knowing that they would all be happy to get to know someone in his life that he could potentially build a serious relationship with.

It was definitely something that gave him an entirely different reason for getting up every day and looking beyond investigating horrendous criminal activity. He focused on Tisha's sweet lips and told her, "You missed a spot."

"Oh, I did…?" Color bloomed on her cheeks.

Glenn took the liberty of using a finger to wipe away the extra chili, then kissed her for good measure and said with amusement, "That's better."

"Yes, it is," she said lightheartedly.

Chapter Ten

After lunch with Glenn, Tisha found the rest of her afternoon quite eventful, to say the least. First, she teamed up with other game wardens to rescue a white-tailed deer after its antlers got entangled in a tree in Shellview County. They succeeded in the endeavor and sent the befuddled deer on its way.

Then Tisha teamed up with Sherman to track down a pair of intoxicated and mischievous hunters, who decided to go on a joy ride with their Honda ATV through a farmer's crops. Lastly, she and her work section boss, Fritz Alvarez, performed a safety check of rafters and boaters along the river.

When she got home, Tisha changed clothes, fed Jacky and then checked in with her mother and father, Goretti and Victor Song. She casually mentioned to them that she had started to see someone. Though expressing surprise, they were elated that she was finally willing to put herself out there again. She felt the same way.

Tisha promised to keep them abreast on how things progressed with Glenn, knowing they were holding out hope that she would someday give them grandchildren to cherish and carry on family traditions. But before she could go there, she needed to know the man in her life was equally committed to having and raising kids as part of their commitment to each other. Was that something Glenn saw in his—or their—future?

That evening, Tisha brought Jacky over to Glenn's house at his invitation. The dogs ran free on the vast property, chasing one another playfully.

"Looks like they're having a good time," Glenn said with a laugh.

Tisha smiled. "I guess they both just needed someone to befriend and exercise with."

"Yeah, I think you're right." He faced her and lowered his chin seductively. "The dogs aren't the only ones looking for lasting friendship and exercise."

"No?" Tisha batted her lashes coquettishly and then, in trying to read him, she asked, "Is that what you're seeking out of this—long-term camaraderie and some physical activity?"

Glenn grinned coolly. "Both seem about right at this point. But, to tell you the truth, I'm hoping things can go a lot further than that over the course of time."

"Good response." Her teeth gleamed at him and Tisha's desire to be with Glenn crept up a few notches.

"I thought so, too." He ran a hand along her jawline. "What do you say, we leave the dogs by themselves for a bit, and we can do our own thing?"

"I say that works for me," she replied, tempering her enthusiasm.

They went inside the house and straight to his bedroom, kissing along the way. After quickly disrobing, Tisha climbed onto the platform bed and beneath the comforter. She watched as Glenn got naked, showing off his nice abs, before he grabbed protection from a three-drawer wooden nightstand and joined her.

Their lovemaking was thorough and demanding, as each yielded to the other's needs, exploring and being explored to their mutual pleasure. It ended with them both exhausted and contented after being victorious in the quest for sexual gratification.

"I think I can get used to this," Glenn whispered sensuously against her cheek.

"Do you really?" Tisha challenged him. "It won't cramp your style as a bachelor having me around—not to mention Jacky?"

"Not even a little." He chuckled. "Especially with Jacky on hand to keep Riley distracted, so I can focus on other things. Or one thing in particular..." He ran his hand down her smooth leg.

"Hmm." She felt a tingle from his touch. "I like the way you think."

"I think a lot about you," he said, pouring on the charm.

"Makes sense, as that works both ways." Tisha had to admit that her thoughts toward him were veering dangerously close to falling in love. Was that something he was ready to hear? Or would going out on a limb at this stage only do more harm than good?

ON TUESDAY MORNING, Glenn sat in a booth at Oliver's Coffee Shop on Quail Street, across from Rhianna Kingsley. They were discussing the latest on the Shellview County Killer investigation, along with the broader agenda for the GBI regional office. That included an ongoing probe into the sexual exploitation of children, an officer-involved shooting and a drug-trafficking case.

Though these other investigations were important in their own right, Glenn was painfully aware that his primary focus at the moment had to remain on solving the serial killer case, with five homicides to date. He understood that the special agent in charge expected no less of him.

"We're looking into every angle here," he assured her while sipping his espresso.

"I don't doubt that," Rhianna said, lifting her cup of chai latte. Her thin eyebrows knitted. "We may need to get the FBI involved," she admitted. "With our resources already stretched thin as it is and the sheriff's department relying on us to take the lead in tracking down the unsub, we could use some extra help here to get the job done."

Glenn bristled at the thought of the FBI getting in the mix and trying to pull rank on him and others from the GBI involved in the case. At the same time, though, he was no stranger to working with the Bureau in partnering on investigations. Or as part of a task force effort. His pride had to take a back seat to solving this serial killer probe.

"Whatever you say," he told her acceptingly. "I won't reject help from the FBI, if that's what it takes to stop him."

Rhianna nodded. "Good. I'll make the call." She tasted her tea. "But just so you know, it's still your case to get to the bottom of—along with the sheriff and her investigators."

"I appreciate the vote of confidence." Glenn met her eyes respectfully. "I'll try not to let you down."

She smiled. "I know that."

He felt that such a time couldn't come soon enough for

both of them in representing the GBI and its role in assisting Marjorie Pierce catch the bad guy.

No sooner had that thought crossed his mind, when Glenn's cell phone rang. The caller happened to be the sheriff.

"McElligott," he answered routinely, glancing at Rhianna.

"Hey," Marjorie said, a catch in her voice. "A 911 call just came in from a man claiming to have strangled to death his girlfriend."

"Really?" Glenn sat up.

"Yep. I'm on my way to his house, even as we speak. Might be entirely coincidental," she continued, "or it could be opening the door to a confession by the alleged Shellview County Killer."

Glenn was left with that disturbing possibility as he disconnected and relayed the information to the special agent in charge.

MARJORIE HAD BEEN making the rounds, per her role as Shellview County sheriff, when she received the call about a possible homicide by strangulation and its potential implications in a serial killer investigation. Before that, her mind had been contemplating next year's election, in which she intended to run for reelection for a third term in office.

It hadn't been an easy decision. Part of her wanted to get beyond being a county sheriff to perhaps running for the board of supervisors in Shellview County. But the fact was that she loved her job and was committed to performing it to the best of her ability. That included cleaning up the streets of illicit drugs, gangs and violent criminal activity. Such as the current case of a serial killer in their midst.

Were they about to nab the unsub? Or not?

Marjorie kept her fingers crossed. She would be happy to solve the murders herself. Short of that, she still welcomed the help of the GBI…and now the FBI, after having brought up the possibility of bringing in the Bureau earlier to Rhianna Kingsley, in wanting to do whatever it took to bring this investigation to a close.

Either way she sliced it, Marjorie was certain that this had to end sooner than later, given the work they were putting in to solve the case. She hoped it was sooner as she pulled her Ford Explorer behind one of her deputies' squad cars, outside a two-story colonial home on Steel Street.

After getting out, Marjorie walked up to the house, where she was met at the door by Deputy Dervla Haddock, a slender twentysomething woman with auburn hair in a piecey cut.

"He's in the living room…" Dervla said tonelessly. "In cuffs with Deputy Winnick keeping an eye on him."

"And the victim?" Marjorie asked.

"Upstairs on the bathroom floor."

"Anyone else inside?"

"No," Dervla told her.

Majorie nodded. "Okay."

Walking inside, she spotted her deputy, Harvey Winnick, tall and bald-headed and in his thirties, standing guard over the suspect, who was seated in a club chair with his hands behind his back. He was white, fortysomething, of medium build and blue-eyed with dark hair in a low fade military-style cut. She noted that he was wearing what looked to be an expensive navy suit and oxfords.

Not too surprising, considering that the residence was located in a high-end neighborhood in town.

Marjorie glanced at the traditional furnishings in the room and back to the suspect and told him, "I'm Sheriff Pierce. And you are…?" She wanted to hear it from him directly.

"Quinn Finnegan."

She peered at him and asked bluntly, "Mr. Finnegan, you want to tell me what you've done?"

He drew a breath and replied matter-of-factly, "I killed my girlfriend."

Marjorie wrinkled her nose and said to the deputies, "Stay with him while I go up and have a look."

She scaled the staircase, went down a long hall and into a spacious and well-furnished primary bedroom, where nothing seemed particularly out of order. Laid out on top of the cane bed were women's underwear, jeans and a floral print T-shirt.

Only when she entered the en suite bathroom did Marjorie spot a naked and slender Hispanic female in her thirties, with long brunette hair, lying on the floor by the bathtub. There was a leather belt wrapped tightly around her neck.

Marjorie turned away for a moment, then looked back at the ruin of a life. As she waited for Glenn McElligott to arrive, she couldn't help but wonder if Quinn Finnegan was guilty of more than one strangulation murder.

GLENN HAD GIVEN Tisha a buzz en route to the crime scene, wanting to let her know that a person of interest had emerged in the Shellview County Killer case. He didn't want to give her false hope that they had their killer. But she also deserved to know where they were, as a witness to an earlier unsolved murder. Then there was the fact that he had grown to trust Tisha as both a confidante and someone he was starting to build a life with outside of work. Apart from their lovemaking being off the charts, they were in sync and it left him wanting more and more.

After reaching the address and going inside, Glenn flashed his identification to the deputies on duty, regarded the handcuffed suspect, who was stone-faced, and headed upstairs, where he found the sheriff in the primary suite just getting off the phone.

"Agent McElligott," she said, acknowledging him, a somber look on her face. "The victim's in there..." She pointed to the bathroom. "It's not a pretty sight."

Glenn stepped into the bathroom and saw the dead woman. She was lying on her back, naked. Her brown eyes were bloodshot on an attractive face and wide open, as if forced to remain that way even in death. He took note of the leather belt that had apparently been used to strangle the victim, as it was coiled around her neck like a snake.

This differed from the type of ligature used to commit the serial murders. Furthermore, he saw no signs of a stun gun being used on the victim. Perhaps the weapon was applied to the back side of her body?

Could the unsub have changed his MO?

Or were they barking up the wrong tree in the joint investigation?

"What's your initial take on this?" Marjorie asked, breaking into his thoughts.

Glenn examined the deceased woman again with his eyes, then responded noncommittally, "Before I answer that, I'd like to speak with the suspect..."

Forty-five minutes later, in an interrogation room at the sheriff's department, Glenn was sitting across from Quinn Finnegan, having already discovered that he was a millionaire hedge-fund manager. The victim had been identified as Naomi Echeverría, a thirty-two-year-old cocktail waitress.

Regarding the suspect steadfastly, Glenn asked him curiously, "Why did you do it?"

Finnegan lowered his head and replied without prelude, "She was cheating on me—and didn't even bother to deny it."

"So you killed her for that, rather than simply man up and find someone else to date?"

"I didn't want anyone else—don't you get it?" he snorted. "I was in love with Naomi. Thought she loved me, too. Guess I was wrong." His countenance contorted. "She laughed in my face." He sighed. "I just lost it…"

"And what exactly did you do in losing it?" Glenn asked for the record.

"I grabbed one of my belts and followed her into the bathroom, where she was about to take a shower…then strangled her."

"What happened next?"

"I went downstairs, calmed down and then called 911," Finnegan responded, eyes lowered as though resigned to his fate as a murderer.

Now comes the more critical part, Glenn told himself, relative to his current investigation. He rested his arms on the table separating them. "Have you made a habit of strangling women, Finnegan?" he asked him point-blank, leaving out the one male victim of the serial killer for the moment.

"Of course not," the man argued innocently. "This is the first time I've taken it to that level with someone... I never imagined I was even capable of doing that, even though I've always had a jealous streak in me."

Glenn leaned forward musingly. "In case you haven't heard, there's been a string of local ligature strangulations over the past six months. Maybe you committed these crimes, too, and added your girlfriend to the list for good measure?"

"I'm innocent of any other killings!" Finnegan insisted. "Whoever you're after, it isn't me."

He said this with such a straight face that Glenn was almost inclined to believe him. But that was hardly good enough. In spite of his reservations to the contrary, Glenn needed more to eliminate Finnegan as a suspect in the Shellview County Killer case.

"We'll need to know your whereabouts during certain days and alibis that can hold up when put to the test," he advised the suspect, while knowing that they would be able to collect his DNA and fingerprints for comparison purposes. He also needed to get a search warrant to examine his cell phone and computer for any info that might come into play.

Quinn Finnegan agreed to this, then was carted off to jail after being charged with the murder of Naomi Echeverría.

THAT EVENING, Tisha was with Glenn as they walked their dogs, held by leashes, down the sidewalk near her town house. Learning that a woman had been strangled and a man had confessed to the murder had shaken up Tisha.

At the same time, she had hoped this was the break they needed to solve the serial killer case.

Unfortunately, it wasn't.

"He's definitely not responsible for any of the serial murders," Glenn told her forlornly. "Quinn Finnegan's alibis checked out. Getting beyond the fact that a different type of ligature was used by the Shellview County Killer, who hasn't been so willing to turn himself in, a preliminary exam of Naomi Echeverría by the associate medical examiner showed no signs of a stun gun being used on the victim. Though Finnegan may not have felt he needed this to overpower his girlfriend, it just doesn't stack up."

"Oh, well..." Tisha muttered, tightening her grip on the leash as Jacky sought to break free. "It wasn't meant to be. But at least Finnegan will be held accountable for killing his girlfriend."

"True, there is that," Glenn said. "And we'll keep plugging away, turning over every rock we can to catch the unsub we're looking for."

I wonder just how long that will take? she couldn't help but ask herself. Would others have to die first before the serial killer was brought to his knees?

"It's all you can do," Tisha agreed, "till he either makes a mistake or we figure out who he is beforehand."

"Yeah." Glenn rounded the corner before she did, with Riley leading the way. "I was thinking that on Saturday maybe we could barbecue some steaks and burgers on my grill, and invite my GBI buddy, Kurt, and that friend of yours you mentioned..."

"Jeanne," she told him. "Yes, that sounds like a terrific idea."

"Cool." He grinned back at her. "We'll do it."

"Should be fun." And a good way, Tisha felt, to integrate their friends into the relationship they were building with each other. If Jeanne and Kurt happened to hit it off, too, as single people, all the better.

Chapter Eleven

Glenn was happy that Tisha had agreed to the Saturday backyard barbecue idea that had popped into his head a few days ago. Seemed like a good opportunity to step away from their respective careers in law enforcement—and the Shellview County Killer investigation, in particular—for some quality time with people they cared about. Though he didn't necessarily want to try to set up his friend Kurt, who was still licking his wounds as a divorcé, the fact that Tisha's friend Jeanne was also divorced and, according to Tisha, available, seemed to Glenn to be a good enough reason for them to decide if it was worth pursuing.

He stood on the outdoor dining limestone backyard patio over a gas-and-charcoal grill combo with a smoker, using a grill spatula to turn over rib-eye steaks and burgers for his guests. Tisha had pitched in by making potato salad and homemade oatmeal-raisin cookies. Riley and Jacky were behaving themselves while seemingly trying to decide if they wanted to walk around gawking or lie down lazily on the grass.

Glenn watched as Kurt broke away from Tisha and Jeanne, who were standing near the edge of the patio in the sunshine, and walked over to him. "Looks like you have a winner in Tisha," he said, grinning, a cold beer in hand.

"You think?" Glenn grinned back, while agreeing wholeheartedly.

"Absolutely. If she's willing to put up with you, you must be doing something right. Or not so wrong."

This brought a laugh from Glenn as he flipped the meat again. "Am I that difficult to deal with?"

"Not at all, buddy." Kurt chuckled. "Seriously, I'm happy for you. All work and no play can get to be boring at times."

"You're telling me." Glenn thought about GBI work and the stress and strain it could bring. It was anything but boring with the range of investigations they dealt with.

"Sorry that it didn't pan out with the strangler you brought in the other day," Kurt said thoughtfully.

"Me, too," Glenn concurred. "Still, it's one less perp to have to contend with."

"Yeah." He put the beer bottle to his mouth.

Glenn glanced at the women and made eye contact with Tisha, who flashed her teeth and seemed eager to play matchmaker, perhaps more than him. "So what do you think of Jeanne?" he asked Kurt.

"Seems like a nice woman," he responded coolly.

"I thought so, too." Glenn smiled, glancing at the good-looking fashion designer. According to Tisha, Jeanne was pretty picky when it came to whom she dated. But maybe Kurt was up to the challenge. "See any opportunities for getting to know each other better?"

"Yeah, the possibilities are definitely there." Kurt took another swig of beer. "We'll see what happens."

"Good luck," Glenn offered supportively, as he started

to put the steaks and burgers on a platter, while being more focused on where things stood with him and Tisha. He believed they were on to something and had no intentions of letting up on that front.

"Too soon to tell," Jeanne told Tisha candidly an hour later as to how she felt about Kurt, as they were clearing the wooden picnic table, while Glenn and Kurt were playing with the dogs. "Right now, I'll settle for a new friend of a friend, and go from there."

"Fair enough." Tisha had no intention of pushing her into anything Jeanne wasn't yet ready for. Each person had to move at their own pace. Or in a different direction.

"Things seem to be clicking nicely between you and Glenn," Jeanne told her.

"They are," Tisha admitted. "He's a great guy."

"And you're great, too!" Jeanne smiled. "So you can't lose."

"I suppose not." Tisha chuckled, though didn't want to be too presumptuous as to where things could go with Glenn. But that didn't mean she would shy away from trying to make it work out in having a future with him.

They joined the men and dogs, and Glenn gave Tisha a hug and kissed her affectionately, then told her, "We'll have to do these get-togethers more often."

"I'd like that," she said, touching her mouth, and gazing at Jeanne and Kurt chatting amiably.

They were about to head back inside the house when Glenn's cell phone rang. He pulled it from the back pocket of his shorts and answered. Tisha saw his expression go from joyful to one of discomfort, as he listened and then muttered, "Okay. I'll see you there—"

Tisha dreaded to ask. "What is it?"

Glenn sighed and said gloomily, "There's been another murder…"

"HER NAME'S PATRICE WHITNEY," Marjorie remarked matter-of-factly, as Glenn stared at the fully clothed body of a slender biracial female in her thirties. She was lying face up in a swamp near Loone Street in Shellview County, surrounded by an abundance of vines and bald cypress trees. Her dark hair was in a feathered mohawk around prominent features. "She was homeless and had been arrested a number of times for loitering and public intoxication," the sheriff said.

"Hmm…" Glenn muttered musingly, glancing at Tisha, who frowned, having insisted on coming with him, though she was off duty and wearing casual clothing. "Not exactly where you would expect to find a homeless person hanging out."

"Definitely not," Marjorie agreed. "Someone obviously brought her here—either while still alive, or dead—and dumped the body."

"Who discovered her?" he asked.

"A couple of hunters. Apparently, they initially thought they were looking at a mannequin." Marjorie rolled her eyes. "But upon closer inspection, realized it was an adult female. My deputies are questioning them further—"

Glenn studied the dead woman again. She was wearing a beige cap-sleeve shirt, ripped wide-leg jeans and black sneakers. He noted that there was a rosemary tattoo on her right arm and a feather tattoo on the other. Looking at her neck area, there were definite signs that she could have been a victim of strangulation.

"I wonder how long she's been here?" Tisha asked.

"Judging by the relatively good condition of the body, I'm guessing not long," Marjorie said.

"I was thinking the same thing." Tisha twisted her lips. "But assuming this is the work of the Shellview County Killer, why would she be killed elsewhere and brought here, where she might not have been discovered for a while, contrary to the other killings?"

"That's a good question," Glenn said. It certainly didn't fit the MO of the unsub serial killer. Could this be an isolated incident? Or an attempt to throw them off guard? Or hide evidence that might lead to the culprit? "I'm sure whoever did this had reasons for doing so. It'll be up to us to flush them out…"

"And we will," Marjorie said, making her intentions clear. "Whatever path that takes us down."

When the associate medical examiner and his team arrived to claim the body, Ned Karakawa wasted little time in giving his preliminary take on the decedent. He said grimly, "Appears as though this was a homicide—using a cord of some type as the ligature murder weapon of choice to strangle the victim." He drew a breath. "There are also marks on her chest that are consistent with the use of a stun gun… As of now, I'd say that death likely occurred elsewhere at some point between thirty-six to forty-eight hours ago—"

The MO is straight out of the playbook of the Shellview County Killer, Glenn told himself. He looked at the sheriff and then Tisha and could see that they had reached the same, and not too surprising, conclusion.

Glenn couldn't help but wonder whether or not this was a new trend by the unsub, in changing his style. Or was it an indication that they were getting too close for comfort in identifying him and he was trying harder to cover his tracks?

"ARENʼT YOU SUPPOSED to be off today?" Fritz Alvarez questioned Tisha. He was standing alongside Sherman near the crime scene, after the DNR had been brought into the investigation by the sheriff's department with the murder occurring inside their work section.

"Yes," she told the sergeant, "but I felt I needed to be here." Even in street clothes, Tisha considered herself to be much more than an interested observer, given the stakes, which she had become part of.

Tisha glanced at Glenn, who backed her up when he said smoothly, "I agree with her. Warden Fletcher's astute insight has proven to be quite valuable in my investigation. We can always use her opinion as we try to solve this latest murder."

Fritz nodded. "That's good to know."

"We're all certainly here to lend our support," Sherman asserted. "And Tisha does have great instincts in everything she does."

She blushed. "Thanks for saying that."

He grinned. "Just speaking the truth. Like Agent McElligott."

Glenn regarded her straight-faced. "Then it's unanimous. Now, we need to get back to the hard work of solving this case—"

"I'm all for that," Tisha said evenly, preferring not to be the focal point of any of them, in terms of being a game warden. On the personal front, though, she was happy to be the center of Glenn's attention, even if she had yet to share having someone in her life with her colleagues.

"We're checking out every entry and exit of the area to see what clues the killer may have left behind," Fritz said.

"Okay," Glenn told him.

Sherman added, "And coordinating our efforts with crime scene investigators to not trip over one another as we search for evidence."

"Nearby surveillance cameras may yield some useful information," Tisha explained, in spite of the rural nature of the landscape.

Glenn rubbed his jaw and said, "What's clear is that whoever killed Patrice Whitney did so with the intention of buying time, while keeping us guessing."

Tisha mulled that over. "I'm guessing that the unsub lured the victim away from wherever she was spending her time—perhaps by offering her food, shelter, or cash— before she realized she had been tricked. By then, it was too late to turn back the clock…"

"Which means we're left with turning the clock ahead to try and beat the unsub to the punch, so to speak, in tracking him down," Glenn stated soundly. "Before some-one else has to end up in a swamp."

Tisha felt a nip in the pit of her stomach at the thought. She also saw this as another opportunity for them to close the gap between the authorities on a mission and an un-relenting serial killer at large, who was more dangerous than ever.

HE WATCHED THEM inconspicuously, reveling in being seen and invisible at the same time. This wasn't necessarily something he had planned from the outset. But then again, some things were meant to be when the circumstances called for it. He had no qualms in having the homeless woman's body found after being given ample time to cover his tracks like footprints in the sand. Quite the contrary, he was counting on the lurid discovery, if only to appease his sense of retribution.

Then there was the unexpected adrenaline rush he got with each kill. As they struggled to breathe while he twisted the cord around their pretty necks, he actually found himself counting the seconds till their breathing stopped altogether. And with each second, he savored the taste of victory and payback, to the extent possible, within his means.

He zeroed in on the good-looking game warden talking with the GBI special agent. They were no doubt discussing the homeless woman's death. And very likely, linking it to the other strangulation murders insofar as means and motive. Good luck with that. He laughed. Getting to the root of it would not be easy. He never intended it to be.

Yet there they were, conferring with each other, hoping to somehow, some way, get inside his head. Wouldn't happen. He was so much cleverer than them. Or any of the law enforcement personnel involved in trying to take him down. Including the FBI.

As it was, his mission wasn't over just yet. He gave the pretty game warden the benefit of his attention again. Soon it would be her turn to feel the life slipping away from chokingly as he wrung her neck till she was dead. And there was nothing that the special agent could do about it. Other than kick himself for not being able to save her.

He chuckled within, pleased with himself. Even while wishing on some level that it had not come to this.

But it had, and he had to live with what he had done and would still do. Till he was through.

It was time for him to leave the scene as easily as he had arrived. He calmly started to walk away. When he approached the sheriff, he gave her a friendly nod and got one in return. The same was true when encountering others who were out to get him, but were too dumb to realize that they had him within their grasp. If only they knew.

Once he was safely beyond the perimeter of the crime scene, he sucked in a deep breath of relief that he had gotten away scot-free. To live to see another day. At which time, he could pick up where he left off, without missing a beat.

That thought captured his fancy and gave him something to look forward to as he reached his vehicle and hopped in, and went on his merry way.

Chapter Twelve

On Sunday, Tisha was at Glenn's place, having spent the night and feeling very much like she belonged, with his encouragement. She was starting to seriously think that what they had was more than just a short-lived romance. Still, until they could talk more about where things stood and could go, she was determined to keep her emotions in check. She didn't want to see them torn apart, just as she had at last opened up her heart again.

They were sitting on a gray sectional sofa in the great room with the dogs resting on the floor as Glenn played his guitar. Tisha loved listening to him and dreamed of getting a piano again, to play in harmony with him.

But at the moment, she found herself thinking about the latest person believed to have become the sixth victim of the Shellview County Killer.

Patrice Whitney.

Why did the killer choose to go after her? Did they cross paths? Did something stand out that drew her to him? Or was it the other way around?

Were these dynamics the same with the other victims?

"I have a cousin named Patrice," Tisha mentioned casually.

"Really?" Glenn looked at her curiously.

"Yeah. As kids, we used to pretend to be one another, after discovering that both names were derivatives of Patricia."

"Cool." He smiled but continued to play a country music song on the guitar.

For whatever reason, the Patricia connection prompted Tisha to use her cell phone to look up online other variations of the name.

There was Pat, Patti, Patty, Pattie, Patsy, Patrina, Patrice, Patrycja, Patrizia, Trecia, Tresha, Tricia, Trish, Tris, Trisha.

On the male side was the name Patrick.

Tisha pulled up the names of the victims of the Shellview County Killer:

Patsy Dunnock.

Walt Patrick.

Patti Arnaz.

Tris Lindberg.

Patrina Morse.

Patrice Whitney.

Hmm. That's odd, Tisha told herself uncomfortably. What were the odds that all the victims would happen to have names that were offshoots, spinoffs, or whatever, of the name Patricia? Just like her own?

She looked them over again and then cast her eyes upon Glenn, who, sensing something was up, suddenly stopped playing and asked tentatively, "Something on your mind...?"

"Actually, there is," she said, hesitant to go further. "Look, this is probably going to sound ridiculous, but I think I may have found something that could connect all the Shellview County Killer victims in an odd way—"

"Okay." His eyes pinned to hers. "I'm listening."

She drew a breath. "I told you about my name and my cousin Patrice's name being versions of the name Patricia?"

"Yeah... Go on..."

"Well, out of curiosity and maybe a gut instinct, I decided to check out other derivatives of Patricia and found that each victim of the serial killer—including the male victim—has a form of the name Patricia, leading me to think that there may be some symmetry here that goes beyond random—" She watched him contemplating this and, while doing so, showed him the names on her phone, as if he needed any help remembering them.

"Hmm... I admit this is weird," Glenn said after a long moment. "But it does seem a bit of a stretch to think that a killer would purposely handpick victims with a range of versions of the name Patricia. And in the case of the male victim, Walt Patrick, given that Patrick is his surname, that makes it seem even more unlikely. Especially when coupled with his girlfriend, Patti Arnaz, being a victim, too. How would a serial killer even begin to have targeted two Patricia namesakes of sorts in one kill? Then there's the fact that Patrina Morse is from Australia. How would the unsub have found her so quicky—if targeting his victims by name—given that she'd only been in Georgia for three days before being attacked?" Glenn took a breath. "The chances of making this work by lining up potential victims with the same name in Shellview County would seem to be astronomical."

"You'll get no argument from me there," Tisha agreed, when thinking about it squarely. "It does appear to be unlikely for even the shrewdest serial killer to be able to orchestrate. Maybe I am way off base here," she added, petting Jacky, who had hopped up next to her on the sectional. "But then again, who's to say that this killer isn't more resourceful than most in locating victims with some version of the name Patricia? Maybe this was his mother's name. The unsub could have decided to get his payback at long last after years of being abused by her as a child or something. Or maybe it's his weird way of taking revenge against a wife, girlfriend, friend, or coworker with the name while not having to own up to it. I'm just saying…"

Glenn chuckled. "Sounds like you've been watching way too many movies or reading crime novels." Before she could respond, thinking that he wasn't taking her seriously enough, even with her having second thoughts, he said levelly, "On the other hand, there may be some merit to your theory worth checking out…"

Her eyes grew with interest. "Really?"

"Yes. In fact, there was a case a few years ago in which a serial killer strangled to death eight women named Linda with an *i* or Lynda with a *y*—the latter being his mother's name—for the very reason you imagined. She'd apparently been abusing him for years, before abandoning him, giving him more reason to exact his warped revenge."

"So we could be looking at the same thing here?"

"Maybe." Glenn leaned back, thoughtful. "The two versions of Lynda would have been easier to pull off. Patricia variations as victims, not so much. But given that our unsub is still on the loose and we obviously haven't connected enough dots to expose him and bring him in, this is certainly an angle that should be looked into."

"Thanks." Tisha gave a sheepish grin. "It may be an entirely overactive imagination on my part, but this some-

how entered my head as entirely plausible, when thinking about my cousin, Patrice…" Her voice lowered an
octave. "Seriously, I hope the killings have nothing to do
with the Patricia approach. Especially since Tisha also
falls into the name variations, so it would mean that my
life could well be in danger, too…" The thought hit her
all of a sudden like a strong gust of wind, sending panic
reverberating through Tisha.

Glenn's eyebrows joined. "Don't even go there," he
scolded her. "Whatever the unsub's motivation or plans
for attack, and who he may be targeting, I'm not about to
let him harm you…threatening everything that's working between us—"

"Neither am I," she insisted, not wanting to see them
lose momentum, either. Tisha started to regain her courage. "As a game warden who knows how to use a firearm and has taken self-defense classes, I won't go down
without one hell of a fight, should I encounter the unsub."

A grin played at one corner of Glenn's mouth. "I don't
doubt that for a moment." The grin went away. "Still, until
we can eliminate your theory altogether, keep your eyes
open and your guard up."

Tisha smiled, feeling grateful for his concern and support. "I will," she promised, putting her hand on his.

"Good." Glenn met her eyes soulfully and Tisha knew
then that he was someone she could count on through
thick and thin, no matter which way their romantic relationship went over the course of time.

ON MONDAY MORNING, Glenn assembled everyone in the
conference room in the sheriff's department for an update,
in addition to welcoming the FBI to the team. He knew

that the Bureau wanted the same thing he did at the end of the day—to put the brakes on a serial monster who was plying his trade in Shellview County to the tune of six victims and counting, if the unsub had his way.

Foremost on Glenn's mind was the notion that the perp could have borrowed a page from serial killer Lucas Conseco and targeted his victims by name. The disturbing thought of Tisha getting caught in the crosshairs of the unsub left Glenn feeling angry and petrified. Now that he had finally found someone who moved him in a way that other women hadn't, giving them both reason for being optimistic when looking ahead, losing Tisha to a serial killer was something Glenn didn't even want to fathom.

He cast his eyes upon her—she was sitting up front, exuding strength and vulnerability at the same time. Her gut instinct in establishing the possible Patricia connection in the case was both impressive and unsettling, to say the least. Yet, the better part of him still felt it was a long shot that the unsub had it in him to be so ingenious and opportunistic to orchestrate that plan successfully.

But long shots still beat the odds in society, Glenn told himself wisely. Even when it came to serial killers. In this case, he couldn't afford to turn his back on any possibility that could lead to a killer.

Using the stylus pen to control what showed up on the monitor, he showed the before-and-after images of the last two victims—Patrina Morse and thirty-four-year-old Patrice Whitney. Morse was blue-eyed and had brunette hair in a collarbone bob, while Whitney had pretty aquamarine eyes and, before the dark mohawk, pink-brown hair in a razor cut. He said equably, "They represent numbers five and six of the persons we believe were the ligature

strangulation victims of an unknown serial killer. Whitney, described as occasionally homeless, was discovered
on Saturday afternoon by rabbit hunters in a swamp in the
county. According to the autopsy report, she was strangled to death elsewhere before being brought to the location and dumped there. The associate medical examiner
has estimated that Whitney had been dead twenty-four
to thirty-six hours prior to when she was found, giving
the unsub ample time to hide his tracks and make a clean
getaway. That being said, the autopsy showed that the victim had engaged in sexual activity before her death, and
DNA has been collected. It is still to be determined as
to whether or not this was left behind by her killer and if
we're able to link it to the unsub…"

After going through the particulars of the Morse and
Whitney murders, his obvious frustration illustrated in
the dark tone of his voice, Glenn sucked in a deep breath
and glanced at Tisha, then put the names of all the victims
on the screen, and said evenly, "In leaving no stones un-
turned in this investigation, Game Warden Tisha Fletcher
has presented an intriguing theory that the victims may
have been chosen for their names, as all have some version of the name Patricia." Glenn paused to let that sink
in, eyeing Marjorie Pierce after he had already run it by
the sheriff, who was skeptical but open-minded to the
possibility. "As you can see, the victims' names do lend
themselves to known variations of Patricia—including
Patrick, the male equivalent, as a victim's surname. While
this could all be entirely happenstance—and admittedly,
it would take some doing on the part of the unsub to line
up the victims to fit the bill—it needs to be explored in

the course of the investigation as we would any possible new leads or directions…"

Glenn put up on the screen a diagram with arrows connecting one victim to another and the final arrow leading to the unsub. "Between the GBI, FBI and sheriff's department, as a task force, we'll work overtime to do what we need to do to see if there's anything here…or if we need to continue to pursue other leads to help crack the case. As for the former, we'll investigate any possible links to anyone named Patricia in and around Shellview County, through social media, surveillance videos, cell phone records, et cetera, utilizing the Georgia Cyber Crime Center, Georgia Information Sharing and Analysis Center, GBI Polygraph Unit and supportive specialized units and resources within the sheriff's department and the Bureau—"

After finishing up, Glenn turned it over to Marjorie, who made it clear right off the bat. "We're not going to stop till the unsub's either in police custody or dead…" She then doubled down on his willingness to tackle any and all possibilities, while zeroing in on some of the more down-to-earth investigative practices, such as forensic examination of footprints and tire tracks found in and around the swamp, and victim movements prior to death, in hopes of finding the break needed to nab the killer.

"That seemed to go relatively well," Tisha commented after they had separated themselves and stepped outside, where the skies were cloudy.

"I think so," Glenn concurred.

"You think the Patricia hypothesis will resonate with others investigating the serial murders?"

"Yeah, I do—at least insofar as a willingness up and down the line to go with the flow and follow each and every lead, no matter how improbable. Believe me, no one wants to get this one wrong. The stakes are way too high."

"I'll say." She looked at him. "I just hope the stakes don't go even higher in the body count, whether those targeted have a version of the name Patricia or not."

"We're definitely on the same page there," he assured her, knowing that to feel otherwise wouldn't correspond with being in law enforcement and trying to nip any case in the bud before it spiraled dangerously out of control.

"Just *there*?" Her lashes fluttered playfully.

He chuckled. "Much more than that. The synergy between us is amazing and keeps growing."

"Good response," she told him with a little giggle.

"So, on that note, shall I swing by your place after work?"

"Sounds great." Tisha touched his arm. "Unless you'd rather I come to you?"

"Whichever." He put his hand on hers. "As long as we get to hang together."

She smiled. "See you, then, at my place. And please bring Riley along. Jacky has grown rather fond of him and gets ornery now when Riley's not around."

Glenn laughed. "In that case, we'll make sure that they get to spend as much time together as possible." In his book, that could mean a very long time, if things continued progressing the way they were between them.

"Perfect." She lifted her chin and dared him to give her a quick kiss.

He was happy to oblige, feeling comfortable to show anyone who cared to see that they were now officially a couple.

Chapter Thirteen

Glenn split from Tisha and hopped in his Dodge Durango for the drive back to his office with renewed intensity, both for solving the current case and building something special with her. Not necessarily in that order. He had always been into his career—the good, the bad, even the unexpected—but Tisha had given him a whole new reason for wanting so much more with his life. She seemed to want the same at this stage, in moving beyond being a widow living in the past, to forging ahead and embracing the bright future she could have.

When his cell phone rang, he lifted it off the seat and saw that the caller was his sister, Josette. Grinning, as he assumed she was merely checking in on him, he put her on speakerphone and placed the cell in the holder on the dashboard. "Hey, sis," he said spiritedly.

"Hey, you," she returned. "Hope I didn't catch you at a bad time?"

"You didn't." At thirty-five, Josette was only three years his senior, but Glenn had always looked up to her as being older and wiser than her years. "What's up?"

"Just wanted to make sure you were still in the land of the living, as I hadn't heard from you in a while."

"Sorry." He gave a little laugh. "I'm still here. I've

been meaning to call…" If that wasn't the lamest clichéd excuse for his neglect. She had a right to be pissed in a sisterly way.

"Yeah, right." She chuckled. "You're forgiven, Mr. Busy GBI Special Agent."

"Thanks," he said sheepishly, while watching the road. He shifted the onus on her. "So bring me up to speed on things."

He listened while she gave a short summary of being in love with her longtime girlfriend, Zoey, and dishing out some great meals as an award-winning chef. After hinting that a marriage could be forthcoming, Josette told him, "We'd love to have you visit again. There's always a room at our place with your name on it."

"I'll keep that in mind," he said agreeably, and added teasingly, "but just so you know, that room should be big enough for two…"

"You're seeing someone?" Surprise filled her voice. "Do tell?"

"Yeah. Tisha's a game warden."

"That's cool. Is it serious?"

"I think so." A grin played on his lips. "And, yes, she'd love to meet you and Zoey."

"Then we need to make it happen, little brother," Josette insisted.

"We will," Glenn promised, and they exchanged a few pleasantries about their parents before disconnecting. He recalled that Tisha had expressed an interest in visiting Alaska. Now, the opportunity was there to do just that. He looked forward to that next big step toward building bridges between their families.

When he got to his desk, Glenn called Layla Ramaswamy at the Crime Lab for an update on DNA taken from Patrice Whitney. "Any news?" he asked when Layla picked up for a video chat.

"Actually, I was just about to contact you," she said enthusiastically. "There is news…"

"I'm listening."

"Well, we took the recovered biological evidence left on Ms. Whitney and submitted the DNA profile to CODIS, where there was a hit!"

"Really?" He gazed at her with interest. "Go on…"

"The DNA is from a Roy Gallagher," she said. "He's been in and out of jail, mostly on drug-related offenses." Layla paused. "He was definitely engaged in sex with the murdered victim shortly before she was killed—"

"Thanks, Layla," Glenn said. "I'll take it from here…"

"You're welcome." She licked her lips. "If he killed her—and the others—I hope Gallagher goes down."

"We'll see what happens."

After hanging up, Glenn immediately went to his laptop to gather as much information as he could on the suspect. He quickly learned that Roy Gallagher was a forty-year-old military veteran, who'd served in Iraq and Afghanistan, before being discharged. Never married, he'd recently been living on the streets and in homeless shelters in Shellview County. Was this how he intersected with Patrice Whitney? And killed her?

For that matter, had Gallagher somehow been able to use his lack of housing to camouflage being a serial killer?

This was something Glenn intended to find out.

THAT AFTERNOON, Tisha taught a class to educate visitors on wildlife laws and proper safety practices, along with Sherman, at the Manikeke Environmental Education Center on Dusty Springs Street in the Manikeke Crossing WMA. It was perhaps her favorite part of being a game warden— offering the public the tools needed to make the most of the rich natural environment and resources at their disposal. If that wasn't enough, it helped to take her mind off less desirable things, such as having to cope with a ruthless serial killer in their midst. Fresh thoughts rolled into her mind about discovering the body of Tris Lindberg.

During an intermission, Sherman folded his arms and asked her in an earnest tone, "So what's up with you and Agent McElligott?"

Tisha fluttered her lashes boldly. "If you're asking if Glenn and I are dating, the answer is yes." She wouldn't hide from her feelings for the man, any more than Glenn wished to do among his colleagues, such as Kurt Stewart.

"That's great." Sherman broke into a smile. "Seems like a nice guy."

"He is," she said and thought truthfully, *And so much more!*

"You're just as nice, which I'm sure he would attest to." Sherman waited a beat and said, "I wish you—and him—the best."

"Thanks." Tisha blushed. "Hope you find someone special, too."

He laughed. "Been there, done that. I'm in no hurry to go down that road at the moment."

"Understood." Only too well. She felt the same way for the longest time after Bradley's death. Then came Glenn and everything changed.

"So you really think there could be something to this

serial killer using different versions of the name Patricia to target his victims?" Sherman asked, cocking an eyebrow.

"Possibly. Who knows?" Tisha tried to downplay it but couldn't shake the feeling that it might not be entirely unfounded. What were the odds that six random victims would all have some variation of the same name? But she also had to admit that the odds of being murdered at all in a single county by a serial killer were long, too. "It only entered my head because the last victim, Patrice Whitney, happened to share the first name of my cousin—an off-shoot of Patricia, as is my own name." That last thought stuck in her throat like a chicken bone. "Checking out the names of the other victims, I realized that they too had variants of Patricia. Whether or not this is entirely coincidental will be up to Glenn and Sheriff Pierce to determine."

"You're right." Sherman gazed at her musingly. "You mentioned that your name also fell into the variations… Never thought of Tisha as being short for or an alternative to Patricia—"

"Now you know," she said with a thin smile.

He furrowed his brow. "You don't think you could be in any danger, do you?"

I can't rule it out, no matter how hard I try, Tisha told herself. She said to him, trying not to freak out, "I hope not. But I'll keep my guard up, just in case." She found herself unintentionally brushing her hand against the Glock pistol in her holster.

"As will I," Sherman said steadfastly. "If this unsub ever decides to come after you, Agent McElligott won't be the only one to have your back."

Tisha gave him a grateful smile for his support. "I appreciate that."

"It's what we do in the DNR," he replied matter-of-factly.

The class gathered again, only this time for some outdoor education with the sun managing to peek out from behind the clouds.

BACKED BY DEPUTIES, FBI agents and a SWAT team armed with Colt M4 carbine semiautomatic rifles, Glenn located the suspect at the Breyford Shelter on Ninth Street, which happened to be a place that Patrice Whitney had been in and out of, according to the sheriff's department.

Glenn made the decision to go in after him. If he was their unsub, there was no way they would allow Roy Gallagher to slip from their grasp. Or hurt someone inside. Or possibly take hostages.

Accompanied by FBI Special Agent Neal Montoya, fiftysomething and thickly built, with gray hair in a taper fade cut and a short beard, Glenn had already removed the SIG Sauer 9mm pistol from his holster. Montoya was holding a Springfield Armory M1911-A1 pistol, and he gave the agent the signal to move in.

As had been indicated by a female undercover sheriff's deputy, posing as a homeless woman for a sneak peek inside the shelter, Glenn found the person of interest seated in a black plastic chair at a wooden dining table against a windowless wall, drinking coffee. Wearing drab clothing and dark tennis shoes, he had a slim build and graying brown hair in a messy man bun.

They moved swiftly across the tile floor toward the suspect, and by the time he turned blue eyes at them, they already had him surrounded, guns pointed, as Glenn barked, "Roy Gallagher…?"

A look of puzzlement crossed his face, as he responded tonelessly, "Yeah, that's me. What is this…?"

"I'm GBI Special Agent McElligott." Glenn set steely eyes on the man. "We need to bring you in for questioning."

"About what?" Gallagher demanded.

"The murder of Patrice Whitney…" he told him sharply.

Montoya introduced himself coldly to the suspect and snorted, "Let's go," while helping Gallagher to his feet.

Half an hour later, Glenn had the suspect in an interrogation room to grill him about what he knew or didn't know about the case.

"Why don't we get right down to business," Glenn said without preface. He was seated across from the suspect, who was cuffed. "Let's talk about Patrice Whitney. She was strangled to death. Did you kill her?" *And ostensibly five other people, as well*, he thought, if this was their serial killer.

"No, I didn't kill her!" Gallagher shot back. "Didn't even know Patrice was dead."

"So you say." Glenn peered at him with skepticism. It didn't surprise him that the suspect was acquainted with the victim. Both had spent time at the same shelter and on the streets, so they were likely to have crossed paths more than once. Still, he had to ask… "But you knew her?"

"Yeah, I knew her," he muttered.

Glenn narrowed his eyes. "We found your DNA on Ms. Whitney's body. You want to explain that?"

Gallagher lowered his head thoughtfully. "We had sex. It was consensual," he insisted.

There had been no indication during the autopsy that the decedent had been sexually assaulted. But it hadn't been ruled out, either, giving Glenn reason to remain suspicious that the suspect could well have engaged in rape and murder. "Too bad she isn't able to verify that."

"It wasn't the first time," Gallagher asserted. "Patrice and I had an understanding."

"And just what was this understanding?" Glenn pressed.

"That we would get together whenever it felt right. I would never have hurt Patrice."

Glenn took that with a grain of salt. "Do you own a car?"

"Do I look like I have a ride?" Gallagher rolled his eyes sardonically. "That's the last thing I need in my life right now."

Glenn considered that he could have been driven to the swamp where she was murdered, but this seemed unlikely. Unless Gallagher had partnered with someone else to commit the crime.

"Someone either kidnapped or coerced Patrice Whitney into going with them, subdued her with a stun gun and strangled her to death with a cord," Glenn stated in a hard tone. "Right now, you're the only one we're looking at as a legitimate suspect. Unless you can—"

Gallagher cut him off as he stated, "You said Patrice was strangled with a cord... Well, I'm afraid that would be a real challenge for me to accomplish. After getting injured in Afghanistan during my last tour of duty, I suffered nerve damage to my right arm. It may look normal on the outside, but on the inside, I can't do much with it. Unless you're suggesting I could strangle Patrice with one hand, you're looking at the wrong dude as her killer—"

Glenn had missed this in checking out the suspect's military background. Would be easy enough to verify and, if so, would make it a tough sell to believe that Roy Gallagher was the culprit in Patrice Whitney's murder. Much less, the other killings attributed to the Shellview County Killer.

By the time he got off work, having conferred with his colleagues in the investigation, Glenn had let Gallagher off the hook for the Whitney homicide, satisfied that the military vet was not responsible for her death.

After picking up a cheese, sausage and pepperoni pizza, Glenn swung by his house and got Riley, before heading over to Tisha's place. She greeted them warmly. As did Jacky, who seemed to like him almost as much as she did Riley.

"Thought I'd bring dinner," Glenn said sweetly, handing Tisha the pizza box.

"How nice of you." She grinned and gave him a peck on the mouth. "I'll get us some plates."

When they were at the table eating, he relayed the latest news about Roy Gallagher, and said regrettably, "Thought we might have been on to something with him, bolstered by the DNA evidence. But it didn't add up at the end of the day."

"I'm sorry, too," Tisha said, while holding a slice of pizza. "Doesn't mean it won't work out the right way the next time." She took a breath. "Has to, sooner or later—"

"You're right, it has to." Glenn bit into his own pizza slice. No matter how many setbacks they had, the investigation was hardly stalled. For one, there was still the possibility that the unsub was targeting victims with name variations of Patricia. Or perhaps some other nonrandom angle they were still missing. He grabbed another slice of pizza and grinned at Tisha as he turned his thoughts to the good feeling he had every time they were together. No matter the background noise of a homicide investigation.

Chapter Fourteen

Shortly after 11:00 a.m. on Wednesday, Tisha was at the gym on an elliptical machine. While doing her best to stay on stride and in rhythm, with a smile, she eyed the woman on the machine next to her, Carole Kitaguchi, who was thirtysomething and petite with dark hair in a topknot, and a regular at the Blair Bay Fitness Center.

Tisha took note that the elliptical on the other side of her was empty, where Jeanne was supposed to be, as they had planned to work out together. Then go for lunch afterward.

So where was she?

Tisha checked her cell phone for any messages from Jeanne. There were none. Could she have forgotten their workout was today? It even occurred to Tisha that maybe Jeanne had been out late with Kurt last night, as they seemed to be getting closer, and overslept. Or lost track of time.

Or just decided to skip the exercise, while being distracted with other things.

I'll give her a buzz after I'm through, Tisha thought, planning to playfully chide her for missing the workout. In reality, she was hoping that Jeanne's excuse was romantic in nature, knowing that her own happiness was reaching a whole new level in her relationship with Glenn. She couldn't wait to see what was in store for them, even as they continued to acclimate themselves to one another. As was true for Jacky and Riley, who were becoming almost inseparable, while ceding their individual territory to one another.

Tisha had just begun to pick up the pace when her cell phone buzzed. Sensing it was important, she stopped and pulled the phone from the back pocket of her capri leggings and saw that it was Jeanne.

Tisha put the phone to her ear and said softly, "Hey."

"Hey. Sorry I'm not there." Jeanne's voice shook. "I'm in the hospital—"

"What!" Tisha spoke louder than she had intended to, drawing the attention of those nearby in the gym. She lowered her voice and asked, "What happened?"

"I was attacked!" she exclaimed. "Someone came up behind me after I left my town house, hit me with a stun gun...and tried to strangle me..."

"I'm on my way," Tisha told her, unnerved, knowing there was only one hospital in Blair Bay.

"Okay." Jeanne's voice broke. "Can't believe this could happen to me..."

Neither can I, Tisha mused, flabbergasted as she disconnected, and turned to Carole, who had stopped exercising.

"What's going on?" she asked curiously.

"Jeanne's been attacked by someone."

Carole's mouth opened with dismay. "Is she okay?"

Tisha took a breath, then admitted dourly, "I don't know." She was so rattled that she hadn't even bothered to ask Jeanne about her physical condition after the ordeal. "I have to go…"

"I understand." Carole put her hand on Tisha's arm. "Let me know what you find out."

Tisha nodded. "I will." She took off, praying that Jeanne would get through this in relatively good shape, while eager to learn more details about the assault and whoever was behind it.

Once she reached her car, Tisha phoned Glenn with the devastating news. "Jeanne was the victim of an attack—" she told him on speakerphone.

"I know," he said somberly. "I just got word on it from Kurt. He witnessed the whole thing…"

"Really?"

"Yeah. He was meeting Jeanne at her place to accompany her to the Blair Bay Fitness Center for a workout, when Kurt saw the assailant go after her. Kurt managed to scare him off, but not before the creep used the stun gun on her and attempted to strangle her. Kurt took her to the hospital to get checked out, but it seems like she'll be alright. I was about to call you with all this when I got your call."

"I'm on my way to the hospital," Tisha told him, as she drove down Ketchan Street. She felt relieved that Jeanne was not seriously hurt. Thankfully, Kurt was on hand to prevent what could have been a tragic outcome. Still, she wanted to be there for Jeanne to offer moral support and get peace of mind on her condition.

"So am I," Glenn said. "I'll see you there."

"Okay." Disconnecting, Tisha focused on the road, even while contemplating if, in fact, Jeanne had been a victim of the Shellview County Killer. If so, it would seem to debunk her name theory for the victims of the unsub. Which still wouldn't make her feel any better that her friend had been accosted by someone who intended her bodily harm.

Ten minutes later, Tisha pulled up to Blair Bay General Hospital on Youngton Street and parked, then raced inside. It had been one of those days she dreaded, when someone she cared about had been put in harm's way. The saving grace this time was that Jeanne would apparently pull through—no thanks to the creep who assaulted her.

Tisha shuddered at the thought as she went to Jeanne's room and found her lying on the bed, with Kurt sitting beside her.

"Hey, you two," she said to them with a strained smile.

"Hey, Tisha," Kurt said, looking beat.

Jeanne sat up. "You really didn't need to cut short your exercise," she said.

"Don't be silly," Tisha replied. "After what happened, I wanted to make sure you were okay for myself, in spite of Glenn indicating as much."

"I see." Jeanne offered her a smile. "Thanks for coming. The doctor should be here any moment, but other than being a bit shaken up, I'm fine. Fortunately, no broken bones or anything."

"That's good to know."

Kurt stood and said, "Why don't I go get us some coffee?"

"Good idea," Jeanne said, and they ordered theirs black and watched him leave the room.

Tisha moved up to the bed and gave her a hug. "Toiling away on the elliptical machine wasn't the same without you," she joked.

Jeanne laughed. "Oh, really?"

"Even Carole took notice and just wasn't herself." Tisha couldn't help but giggle.

Jeanne winced. "Sorry. Guess I'm still feeling the lingering effects from the stun gun."

Tisha furrowed her brow, envisioning being made to feel disoriented and totally helpless. She sat on the bed and demanded, "Tell me everything that happened—"

NEEDLESS TO SAY, the disturbing news that Jeanne Rutland had been attacked in broad daylight, outside her town house, threw Glenn for a loop. The fact that it was just a few homes down from Tisha's place was even more unsettling. Was this coincidence or what? Could the attacker somehow have mistaken Jeanne for Tisha, in fitting in with the Patricia angle? Or had Jeanne been the intended target all along? If the unsub was their serial killer, it would indicate, more or less, that the names of the victims were coincidental and nothing more.

After arriving at the hospital, Glenn left his vehicle in the parking lot and went in, making his way to the emergency department, where Jeanne was in an exam room.

In the corridor, he ran into Kurt, who was holding a tray with three coffees, and muttered to Glenn, "Hey."

"How's she doing?" Glenn asked.

Kurt, looking grim-faced, replied, "About as well as could be expected after being attacked—" He drew a breath. "The doctor's looking her over now."

"Did you get a good look at Jeanne's attacker?"

"Not really, other than he was white, tall and wearing a blue zip hoodie with the hood over his head." Kurt set his jaw. "Honestly, the moment I saw the perp on top of her, I was mostly concerned for Jeanne's safety. I yelled at him and ran toward them. That's when he got off Jeanne and sped away on foot."

"Okay." Glenn patted him on the shoulder understandingly. "I need to talk to Jeanne."

Kurt nodded. "This way…"

Glenn followed him to the room, then stepped inside and saw Tisha standing off to the side as Jeanne sat on the bed while being examined by the doctor, a thirtysomething Hispanic female with short dark hair.

"Everything checks out," the doctor said. "Other than some soreness to your neck and a few bruises from falling to the ground, you should be fine."

Jeanne grinned. "That's good to know."

"The puncture marks from the stun gun will go away over time. Over-the-counter pain medication should relieve any discomfort, if needed."

"Thanks, Doctor Hernandez," Jeanne said.

"Always here to help," she told her, offering a smile.

Glenn introduced himself to the doctor in his professional capacity, glad that she was able to provide assistance to her patient, and watched as she left the room.

"Guess we didn't need hospital coffee after all," Kurt quipped, while handing a Styrofoam cup to Jeanne and Tisha.

"It was sweet of you to get some, nevertheless," Jeanne told him, taking a sip of coffee.

"Thanks," Tisha said, moving closer to the bed.

Glenn did the same and said, "Glad you're alright."

"You and me both." Jeanne made a face. "Never saw that coming…"

That's true with most crime victims, he told himself realistically, but said to her, "I need to ask you some questions about the attack."

"Can't that wait till she's home?" Tisha queried.

"It can," Glenn allowed, glancing at her and then Kurt, "but it's important that we get as much information as we can on the crime while it's most fresh on her mind."

"It's fine," Jeanne insisted, as she remained seated. "Let's just get this over with. I'll tell you whatever I can..."

"Okay." Glenn wanted to keep this as delicate as possible, yet could not afford to go too soft, given the stakes. Jeanne could be the first target to survive the serial predator known as the Shellview County Killer. Even then, Glenn knew that she would likely need to come in for a formal statement later. "What can you tell me about the person who attacked you, by way of description, clothing, what he may have said to you—anything that comes to mind...?"

"It all happened so fast—" Jeanne pressed her hand on the examination room bed. "Definitely an adult male, perhaps in his thirties, tall and sturdily built. He came up from behind me, seemingly out of nowhere, and zapped me with the stun gun. Couldn't really make out his face as I went down, but could tell that he had on glasses, wore a hood over dark hair and was wearing dirty jeans." She sighed. "Before I knew it, he had jumped on me and put his hands to my neck. Thought I might pass out, but he released me when Kurt showed up, and the man stormed off. I think I heard a car, but since I was disoriented from the stun gun, it could have been my imagination..."

I'll have to see if surveillance cameras picked up cars leaving the area around the time the crime occurred, Glenn told himself. He then pondered the notion of the perpetrator trying to strangle her with his bare hands rather than with a cord, as was the case for the serial killer's victims. Had the unsub chosen a different method because he'd panicked, due to the nature of the audacious attack? Or had he thrown his playbook out the window as the desire to kill intensified? Glenn also had to consider the possibility that this was an isolated attack, unrelated to the other incidents.

"Have you had any reason to believe someone might have been stalking you of late?" he asked her.

"I'm not aware of being stalked by anyone," Jeanne asserted. "But maybe the perpetrator was good enough to keep me from knowing what he was up to."

"That's often the way it works with stalkers, isn't it?" Tisha said, gazing at him.

"Yeah, they often operate surreptitiously," Glenn conceded. "This could just as easily have been an opportunistic attack," he added, considering.

Jeanne frowned. "Does that include being caught in the crosshairs of the Shellview County Killer? If so, how did I get so lucky as to come away from it alive and well, if not shaken from my experience?"

"It's less about luck and more about the timing that had you meeting up with Kurt." Glenn looked toward his fellow GBI special agent, who nodded accordingly.

"He's right," Kurt said, putting his hand on her shoulder. "I'm glad I was around to stop that monster. Just wish I'd gotten there sooner."

She smiled gratefully, "Trust me, I'm not complaining one bit!"

Glenn hated to have to be brutally honest with her, but she deserved that much. "As for the nature of the crime, there's a good chance that you were attacked by this serial killer. Some of the things fit. Others do not," he confessed, and glanced Tisha's way, wondering how she was processing this. "Whoever your assailant is, we'll do everything we can to bring the person to justice."

"That includes getting a forensic sketch artist to work with you in possibly giving us something to help identify and flush out the unsub," Kurt said firmly.

Jeanne tilted her head in his direction. "As I said, I didn't really see his face, other than the glasses—but I'll do my best."

Kurt held her hand. "That's all we can ask."

She gazed at Glenn and asked nervously, "Is he going to come after me again...?"

"I don't think so," he responded with a straight face, making eye contact with Kurt. "Now that the element of surprise has been taken away from the unsub, it's not likely he'd want to take another crack at you and risk capture." That sensible perspective gave way in Glenn's head to the other possibility. A determined serial killer—if this was one—might have an overwhelming need, along with a big ego, to want to finish what he started. They couldn't allow that to happen. "But to be on the safe side, I'll arrange with the sheriff's department's protection unit to offer you security as a witness, till your attacker is brought into custody."

Jeanne nodded. "Thank you."

"In the meantime, you're welcome to stay with me," Tisha offered sincerely.

"I've got this," Kurt told her. "I'll keep an eye on Jeanne for as long as she needs protection."

"That works for me," Jeanne said with a smile.

Glenn could see that Kurt was really into her, just as he was into Tisha. Looked as though all of them were in a good place as far as starting relationships. But first and foremost, they needed to get past the fact that someone had just tried to kill Jeanne. And that Tisha had been swept up into the case in various ways...and was still potentially a target of the killer.

"Let's get out of here," he told them, and got no arguments in leaving the hospital.

THAT EVENING, Tisha walked hand in hand beside Glenn along the beach by the river, with Jacky and Riley up ahead of them playing with each other. The dogs had gotten into a comfort zone with each other that Tisha believed paralleled the one between her and Glenn. She remained positive about where things could go between them, though still wanted to hear more from him on his take on the future.

But for the time being, spending quality time together in the midst of the dangers that seemed to be lurking around them like sharks was something she wouldn't trade for anything.

After padding across the white sand in their bare feet in for a bit, Tisha broke the silence when she asked interestedly, "Do you think the digital sketch of the unsub who attacked Jeanne will yield any results?"

"Some sketches are spot-on, leading to a quick arrest," Glenn told her. "Others may be off-center and could take longer to hit the mark—if they do at all. We're comparing it with surveillance video in the area to see if the stars can align. One can only hope for the best."

Tell me about it, Tisha thought, and said wonderingly,

"I suppose that the attack on Jeanne by, presumably, the Shellview County Killer throws cold water on the culprit targeting people whose names correspond with derivatives of Patricia?"

"Not necessarily." Glenn squeezed his fingers around hers. "Assuming we are talking about the same perp— never mind the different MO from other victims and failure to complete the attempted murder—it's still possible that there was a method to his madness, so to speak."

"Such as?"

"Well, the unsub may have deliberately tried to throw us off in the investigation in feeling the heat, by changing his routine."

"I suppose." Tisha regarded him musingly. "But since the Patricia theory hasn't been made public, as far as I'm aware, how would he suspect we were onto this possible connection with the murders—if that was the reason for him shifting gears?"

"Not sure it has anything to do with the victims' names, per se," Glenn replied frankly, as Riley and Jacky circled around them. "Could be the unsub had his own reasons for targeting Jeanne, in particular. Maybe it was more about an opening that presented itself and he went for it, regardless of her first or last name. Or he could have been stalking her, unbeknownst to her, as perhaps an attempted sexual assault, robbery and homicide all tied into one." Glenn watched as Riley jumped on his leg playfully, and continued, "In any event, whether the unsub decided we were on to him or not, irrespective of public awareness of some details, it's still very much up in the air. For now, we'll have to assume that he's being driven by demons that are largely opportunity-oriented—till we find evidence contrary to that. We'll just have to wait and see where this goes..."

"Fair enough," she said, happy to be in his company in the interim.

Tisha actually hoped that the killings were not name-related, when all was said and done, as it otherwise would mean that she herself remained in the line of fire as a potential target of the unsub. Not a comfortable thought, to say the least. At the same time, she didn't want to be off the mark at the expense of Jeanne being assaulted and nearly killed.

As Jacky got her attention, apparently getting restless away from home, Tisha eyed Glenn and said, "I think the dogs are ready to go."

"Okay, if they insist," Glenn said with a grin, and they turned around and headed back up the beach.

THE SHELLVIEW COUNTY KILLER watched as the DNR game warden and GBI special agent walked along the beach with their dogs, oblivious to his presence. Admittedly, he had begun to warm up to the nickname he'd been given, as it did seem to fit, the more he thought about it. He was, after all, killing those he had chosen to die in Shellview County. The fact that the press had decided to supply him with a handle that was apropos was something he could live with. Even if, at the same time, others were forced to die by way of his actions.

He studied the couple again...with a particular focus on the attractive game warden named Tisha Fletcher. Like her friend Jeanne, she was ripe for the picking. It was unfortunate that the divorcée fashion designer had gotten caught up in something not of her own making, but this was how it needed to be. Some things couldn't be helped. For better or worse. To her good fortune, she had survived her brush with death.

The same would not be true for the game warden. She had to die. Just like the others. And there would be no one standing in his way. Least of all, the special agent. No matter that he had designated himself as her protector. Soon it would be time to do what needed to be done. Only then could he take a breath and appreciate what he had accomplished in exacting his revenge for reasons no one saw coming.

Except him, of course.

He watched with interest as Tisha and Glenn McElligott made their way across the beach, with the dogs now leading the way. Too bad neither animal sensed his presence, or they could have alerted their owners of the danger that was within their midst without them being privy to it.

Their loss would surely be his gain, as he observed them until they disappeared from sight. He headed across the beach in the opposite direction, his clever mind plotting his next steps and how this would end.

The Shellview County Killer laughed to himself even as he felt anger well up inside him like hot air that needed to be released. He found solace in knowing that this would be accommodated soon enough, one way or another.

Chapter Fifteen

The following day, Glenn was in his office on the laptop, studying surveillance video in the area around Tallins Drive, near the town house where Jeanne was attacked. Not to mention, it was uncomfortably close to Tisha's place, giving him more cause for concern and making Glenn even more determined to get to the bottom of this attempted murder.

He was relieved that he wasn't reading another autopsy report on a strangulation victim of the Shellview County Killer. Apart from that meaning someone else had to die, it would also have further emboldened the unsub into thinking he was invincible while looking to add more victims to his list.

Beyond that, Glenn hated the thought of Tisha's friend being killed, just as Jeanne and Kurt seemed to be on track for a romantic success story. *Just like me and Tisha*, Glenn told himself satisfyingly, as he continued to pore over the footage. *We have something really special, no doubt about it*. They, too, deserved happiness, considering that both had fallen short in their previous relationships.

When he spotted a vehicle that sped off on Judson Drive, which ran parallel to Tallins Drive, one street over, it got Glenn's attention. Especially since it occurred shortly after the attack, when the unsub had run off, and in that direction.

Glenn rewound the video and paused on the car, zooming closer. It was a blue GMC Acadia midsize SUV. He couldn't make out the driver, but it appeared to be a male. Turning to the back of the car, Glenn was able to see the license plate clearly enough. He ran the plates and, shortly thereafter, was surprised to see that the vehicle was registered to a Sherman D. Galecki.

As in Game Warden Sherman Galecki? Glenn asked himself. What the hell was he doing in that area at the time Jeanne was attacked, given that his home address had him living miles away in Akerston Heights? Coincidence? Though the description of the unsub was sketchy at best, Galecki seemed to at least fit the general physical characteristics of the man who tried to strangle Jeanne to death.

Glenn couldn't help but think back to a conversation with Tisha in which she tossed out the possibility that the serial killer could be someone inside the DNR. If not the Region 5 Law Enforcement Division itself. Had she been given reason to suspect Galecki?

Had that been true, would Tisha have kept it to herself? He seriously doubted that.

As it was, they had looked into the possibilities in that regard, and there had been no red flags pointing toward anyone in particular at the DNR.

Had they missed the boat here?

I'll refrain from jumping to any conclusions yet, Glenn thought, though his suspicion radar was off the charts. Especially after documenting that a digital license-plate scanner had picked up the SUV moving rapidly away from the area several streets over during the same time frame.

Lifting his cell phone, he rang Tisha for a video chat. Momentarily, her lovely face appeared on the screen. "Hey," he said.

"Hey." She flashed a thin smile. "What's up?"

"What can you tell me about Warden Sherman Galecki?"

"Sherman?" Tisha frowned curiously. "Well, for starters, last year he was named by the DNR as Game Warden of the Year."

"Is that so?" Glenn was admittedly impressed. But that still didn't give him a free pass from being capable of committing murder. "What else?"

"Let's see…" She mused. "He's obviously good at what he does. Was in a long-term relationship till recently. Keeps mostly to himself on the job, but is still friendly toward others when he wants to be."

"I see." Glenn let that sink in. Seemed like a stand-up kind of guy. Didn't mean there wasn't a very dark layer beneath the facade.

Her eyes widened suspiciously. "Why are you asking about Sherman?"

Glenn paused and thought, *How do I put this without indicting her colleague prematurely?* "Galecki's personal vehicle was spotted leaving the area around the time Jeanne was attacked," he said bluntly.

"Really?" Tisha's voice rose with incredulity. "Hmm…"

"I'm sure Galecki has a legitimate reason for being there," Glenn offered politely, "but like me, he lives in Akerston Heights. Do you know if he knows anyone in your neck of the woods, besides you?"

"Not that I'm aware of," she admitted thoughtfully. "But we aren't really that close or anything, so I couldn't tell you why he was in Blair Bay at that time." She made a face. "I'm sure he can explain himself."

"I hope so." Glenn still wondered about the game warden and if he could possibly be doubling as a would-be killer and serial killer all at once. "When you discovered the body of Tris Lindberg, did Galecki appear genuinely surprised?"

Tisha pondered his question, then answered, "Yes, it seemed so." She paused. "Do you really suspect Sherman of having something to do with her death? Or attacking Jeanne…as a serial killer?"

"I'm not pointing any fingers at this point," he told her candidly. "But we have to look at everything and everyone that manifests itself in the investigation. As it is, Galecki had access to and knowledge of most—if not all—the places where the serial murders occurred. Now, a car registered to him happens to be fleeing the scene shortly after Jeanne was attacked. This may be totally coincidental, but it certainly gives me pause. Only Galecki can clear this up."

"When do you plan to talk to him?" Tisha asked.

"This morning," Glenn said matter-of-factly. "I'll ask Galecki to meet me at the sheriff's department for routine feedback on the investigation as a game warden, so he'll have his guard down, just in case things go south along the way."

"Okay." She was thoughtful. "I'd like to be there. If Sherman could really be this horrible creature, I want to see him fess up. Also, my presence could defuse the situation, if it should come to that."

"I understand. You're more than welcome to come. If this is a nothing burger, all the better. It would just be a short hiccup." Glenn narrowed his eyes. "But if Galecki has something sinister to hide, he'll need to be held accountable."

"I agree," she said evenly.

Though he wasn't entirely comfortable with her being anywhere near Galecki if he was guilty of assaulting Jeanne—as well as committing multiple homicides— Glenn understood Tisha's point of view as his colleague. *I'll make sure she's kept at a safe distance while he's being interrogated*, Glenn told himself.

After they disconnected, he ran this by the special agent in charge and Rhianna agreed that they needed to jump on it. He then called the sheriff, explaining the circumstances, and Marjorie was also on board and ready to do whatever was needed in the investigation.

HONESTLY, TISHA WASN'T quite sure what to expect as she watched on the video monitor alongside Sheriff Pierce as Sherman entered the interrogation room under the guise of a friendly conversation about assisting with the investigation. Only it was far more than that, unfortunately, with greater implications for him. Jeanne's vague description of the unsub had hardly described Sherman as her assailant. Nor had Kurt seen enough of his face to describe him accurately.

But the general description of the attacker did not exclude Sherman. To this, Tisha was left to wonder if someone she worked with could possibly have been a serial killer, right under her nose. Had he actually known in advance where Tris Lindberg would be found in the Manikeke Crossing and was merely putting up a good front as a law enforcement game warden? Was the same true for the other murders attributed to the so-called Shellview County Killer?

Why would he have gone after Jeanne, who didn't fit the Patricia-named derivatives of the other victims? And was the attempted strangulation with his hands, rather than a ligature, meant to throw off the investigation? Or was it a sign of desperation by someone intent on killing by any means necessary?

That still brought it all back to whether or not Sherman was the unsub, hidden in plain view. Till now.

Guess I'm about to find out, Tisha told herself, as she watched Glenn step into the room in what could well be the break they had been looking for in the case. Or a misdirection that was playing into the hands of the real culprit.

GLENN KEPT HIS cool as he shook Sherman Galecki's hand, while trying to keep an open mind about the man. Per standard procedure, Galecki had to temporarily give up his service firearm while in the sheriff's department.

"Thanks for coming in," Glenn told him as he sat across from him at the table.

Sherman looked frazzled as he touched his glasses and said, "No problem. How can I help?"

"We're looking into the attempted murder of a woman that occurred yesterday morning in Blair Bay on Tallins Drive."

The game warden cocked an eyebrow. "Are we talking about Tisha?"

"No, thankfully," Glenn happily reported, while verifying that Galecki was well aware of where Tisha's residence was located. "She does know the victim, though…"

Sherman seemed relieved. "Okay…?"

"As of now, the perp is still at large," Glenn pointed out. He opened the laptop on the table and turned the screen toward him.

"What am I looking at?" Sherman asked, as if clueless.

"Surveillance video picked up this blue GMC Acadia SUV speeding away on a parallel street shortly after the attack on the victim. The suspect was seen running in that direction beforehand." Glenn peered at him. "I ran the plates and discovered that the car belongs to you, Warden Galecki."

"Not sure I like where this is going." Sherman narrowed his eyes and said, "Just what are you asking me, Agent McElligott?"

Might as well get to the nitty-gritty, Glenn thought, and responded straightforwardly, "I need to know why you were in the area at that time. And why you were in such a hurry to get away…"

Sherman sucked in a deep breath and sat back. "It's not what you think."

"Hope you're right," Glenn retorted. "Since the unsub tried to strangle the victim, it has me thinking that it could be the same person we believe has strangled to death six individuals, thus far. If you're innocent, you'll need to convince me here and now. Otherwise, this is not going to end well for you…"

Glenn realized that they had no hard evidence to link Galecki to the attack of Jeanne. Much less, the serial murders. And he deserved the benefit of the doubt. But at this point, there was little room for error. Or second-guessing. For the game warden's sake—and maybe even Tisha's peace of mind as she watched from another room—it was best to play hardball and see which way the pendulum swung.

"Yeah, I was in the area at that time," Sherman admitted, "as the surveillance footage indicates. But it was only coincidental. I had no idea that someone was being attacked one street over." He sucked in a deep breath. "I was visiting a woman I'd been dating off and on. Name's Emily Vanasse. She's a registered nurse at Blair Bay General Hospital. We had a disagreement about where things were going between us. She wanted more of a commitment, I wanted less of one. We broke things off and, feeling flustered, I left her house in a huff. Guess I drove away faster than I should have. I'm sure Emily will vouch for everything I've just said—including providing video from her security system that shows me leaving her place and getting into my SUV and driving off."

"We'll check out your story," Glenn told him, feeling it seemed credible enough. In truth, he was hopeful that someone Tisha worked with daily would not be doing double duty as an attempted murderer and serial killer. But that remained to be seen.

Sherman nodded. "Am I free to go?"

"Yeah, you're free to go," he allowed, knowing they couldn't hold him without just cause. "Just don't go very far till your alibi is verified." Glenn stopped short of demanding that he accounted for his whereabouts during the serial killings. The evidence as yet did not support that the game warden was guilty of anything. Especially if it was proven that he played no part in Jeanne's victimization, with Kurt as an eyewitness to the attack, and neither able to finger Sherman as the unsub.

TISHA FELT SORRY for Sherman, having listened as he defended himself. She had no idea that he'd been seeing someone and that it didn't work out. Not that he owed her an account of his love life. Even if he knew about hers.

Mainly, she just wanted him to be cleared of any wrongdoing against Jeanne. The thought that Sherman would try to hurt—or actually murder—her friend was one that Tisha would just as soon not have. Same was true of the notion that he could be a serial killer. Presumably, the investigation would now move in a different direction.

When they awkwardly ran into each other in the hallway of the sheriff's department, Sherman, who looked like a wounded puppy, muttered, "Sorry to hear about your friend being attacked."

"Me, too."

"I had nothing to do with it."

"I believe you," she told him, trusting her instincts even before verification of his alibi.

Sherman nodded. "Better get out of here before they find another lame excuse for interrogating me."

Tisha smiled thinly. "Catch you later."

She watched him walk away and then went to find Glenn—who was conferring with the sheriff and other investigators—to check on the state of the investigation, now that it appeared Sherman would no longer be the focal point of Jeanne's ordeal.

More troubling to Tisha at the moment was how Jeanne's attack figured into the serial killer case. Could one have absolutely nothing to do with the other? If so, did this keep alive the possibility that her theory on the murders was not so far-fetched after all?

It would mean that a potential target still remained on

her back as someone who fit the unsub's warped philoso-
phy in killing, whatever the actual motivation or reason-
ing may be for his deadly actions.

Chapter Sixteen

In spite of having a feeling that Sherman was likely on the level with his claims of innocence in the attack on Jeanne—to say nothing for his possible role in the serial slayings affecting Shellview County like the plague—Glenn still needed to verify his alibi, in order to eliminate him as a suspect.

He walked down the corridor at Blair Bay General Hospital and approached the curvy nurse in her late twenties with curly chin-length crimson hair, and asked what he already knew the answer to, "Emily Vanasse?"

She looked up at him and responded, "That's me."

"GBI Special Agent McElligott." He showed his identification. "I wonder if I can have a word with you?"

"Sure…" she said tentatively. "Did I do something wrong?"

"No. It's regarding Sherman Galecki."

"Sherman?" She frowned. "What's he done…since I last saw him?"

"Hopefully nothing," Glenn stressed. "Just need you to clear up a couple of things."

"Okay."

"Why don't we step over here?" He indicated an area apart from traffic in the hall. Once there, Glenn regarded her and said straightforwardly, "I'm investigating an attack of a woman on Wednesday morning in Blair Bay. The perpetrator got away. The incident happened to occur shortly before the time in which a vehicle that was driven by Warden Galecki sped off on the next street over."

Emily's eyes widened. "You think Sherman had something to do with the attack?"

"Not necessarily," Glenn suggested, trying to allay Emily's fear for the moment. "Just a routine part of the investigation." He paused. "According to Galecki, he was at your house when the assault occurred—he says he left after you had an argument, and drove off in a hurry. Can you vouch for that?"

"Yes, of course." Her nostrils flared musingly. "We had a fight over his commitment issues and broke up. That's it. He's a jerk and I'm probably better off without him, but Sherman would never intentionally harm a woman… or anyone else, for that matter."

That's good enough for me…almost, Glenn told himself. "When it's convenient, I'll arrange for a sheriff's deputy to drop by your house to check your security video to verify the time."

"Sure, no problem," she agreed. "My shift ends at seven and I can be home by seven thirty."

"Great." He smiled at her. "I'll let you get back to it. Thanks for your time."

She nodded and said, "Whoever attacked her, I hope you find them."

"So do I," he assured her and walked away, feeling as though Galecki had just dodged a bullet.

Meaning that Jeanne's assailant, who was likely a serial killer, was still at large and becoming more brazen than ever.

ON FRIDAY, Glenn got word that another suspect had emerged, with Sherman Galecki off the hook. Surveillance video showed a man matching the physical and clothing description of Jeanne's attacker running into an alleyway close to the time of the attack. This corresponded shortly thereafter with a reported stolen late model Mitsubishi Outlander, believed to have been taken by the unsub. Using facial-recognition technology, the Shellview County Sheriff's Department identified Jimmy McPhail, a forty-two-year-old ex-con, as a person of interest. A BOLO alert was issued for the car and McPhail.

When the car was found abandoned near a convenience store on Kellem Road in a rural part of the county, GBI crime scene investigators processed it for evidence. Latent prints were retrieved and put into the automated fingerprint identification system, leading to a positive identification of McPhail.

"He couldn't have gone far," Glenn told Sheriff Pierce after they had joined other investigators at the scene, in what was believed to be a positive development in both the attempted murder of Jeanne Rutland and the overall Shellview County Killer investigation.

"I agree," Marjorie said, having dispatched the department's drone unit to scour the region, along with having a SWAT team and a crisis negotiation unit on hand to deal with the situation. "We'll find him."

To Glenn, this pretty much went without saying. If McPhail was their unsub, allowing him to slip through their fingers wasn't an option. With the close call for Jeanne and the likelihood that it was tied to the serial murders of six other individuals, it was imperative that they bring the suspect in before more harm could come to others.

When it came across the radio that a body, believed to be that of Jimmy McPhail, had been located behind a nearby abandoned farmhouse, Glenn wasted little time hopping in his Dodge Durango Pursuit and following the sheriff's Ford Explorer toward the address on Lyman Road. The last thing he had wanted was for the suspect to die before being interrogated.

After arriving at the scene, Glenn made his way past deputies and other law enforcement personnel, overgrown weeds and the dilapidated farmhouse, to the backyard, where he spotted the corpse of a tall and muscular man in his early forties lying on his back on brown grass. A pool of blood encircled his short black hair and there was a cut on his chin. He was wearing glasses, a blue zip hoodie, dirty jeans and dark-colored tennis shoes. The clothing corresponded with Jeanne's description of what her attacker was wearing.

Glenn noted the subcompact 9mm handgun lying by his side, the dead man's thick fingers clutching it, as Marjorie stated presumptively, "Looks like McPhail chose to check out, rather than turn himself in."

"Yeah." Glenn sighed. "Too bad. There's still a lot of unanswered questions he's taken to the grave with him."

"We'll try to get as many of those questions answered as possible," the sheriff remarked, "once we can get a look at his cell phone, computer and residence to gather evidence…"

"Can hardly wait," Glenn muttered humorlessly. He happened to spot something beneath the dead man that caught his eye, prompting him to don a pair of disposable nitrile gloves to check it out. He squatted down and carefully pulled out a mini stun gun that must have fallen out of the suspect's pocket upon impact. "This might answer one question in connecting the dots between McPhail, Jeanne and the other victims of a serial killer…"

"Indeed." Marjorie nodded, then opened a plastic evidence bag for him to drop the stun gun in. "We'll get this processed right away, along with what looks like a ghost gun."

"I think you're right," Glenn concurred, gazing at the firearm again, knowing that privately made firearms, or PMFs, were hard to trace and therefore popular among offenders.

As crime scene investigators moved in and a team from the medical examiner's office arrived, Glenn stepped away, along with Marjorie, to assess the situation and what looked to be the biggest break yet in the case.

With the deceased positively identified as Jimmy McPhail, Glenn and other authorities, armed with a search warrant, raided a second-story apartment on Twenty-third Street in Baldwin County, Georgia, where McPhail lived. Potential evidence confiscated from the modestly furnished one-bedroom unit included a roll of twine cotton cord. There was also crack cocaine, fentanyl, heroin and drug paraphernalia recovered, as part of the dark picture being painted of the man believed to be the Shellview County Killer.

"LOOKS LIKE WE'VE identified the perp responsible for attacking Jeanne and strangling to death six people," Glenn told Tisha later that day, as they were walking the dogs.

"Really?" She eyed him interestedly as he held Riley's leash steady. It was music to her ears and would be to Jeanne's as well, no doubt, as someone who had managed to survive the killer, against the odds.

"The pieces have come together to support that contention," he told her. "Jimmy McPhail had a stun gun that was apparently the one used on Jeanne and the other victims. The GBI Crime Laboratory revealed that the roll of cotton cord found at McPhail's apartment was consistent with fibers collected from around the necks of the victims and their clothing. Then there's surveillance video at various locations that showed someone fitting McPhail's description lurking around, coming or going." Glenn took a breath. "It appears that McPhail, took his own life as we were closing in on him, rather than be a man and face justice," he said with dissatisfaction. "We ran the ghost gun he used through the ATF's National Tracing Center and National Integrated Ballistic Information Network, from which we learned that the firearm had been used to commit crimes in Georgia, South Dakota and Michigan."

"Wow!" Tisha was relieved that McPhail hadn't used the gun to shoot Jeanne. She may never have recovered. "Thank goodness he'll no longer be able to terrorize Shellview County, whatever his rationale was for the killings," she added, realizing that they might never know if there was any merit to the Patricia perspective. *Probably just the luck of the name draw*, she decided, given that Jeanne's name did not correspond with that theory.

"I was thinking the same thing." Glenn grinned at her, as though reading Tisha's mind.

"Hmm…" She looked at the man she had fallen in love with and wondered if he felt the same way about her. His body language may have said one thing. But until the words came from his mouth, she wouldn't presume to speak for him. Instead, she said awkwardly, "So where do we go from here...?"

He seemed to give that a long moment of consideration, then responded in an ambiguous way, "Wherever our hearts desire..."

She couldn't let him off that easily. "What does your heart desire?" she asked directly, ignoring Jacky pulling on the leash to get her attention.

Glenn gazed at her as he answered smoothly, "You and only you, Tisha."

She couldn't help but blush at his earnest response. Though she would have liked to hear more on his feelings, Tisha didn't want to press the issue. Right now, she took delight in knowing he seemed totally committed to her and what they were developing between them.

At the moment, that would have to do.

It was obvious to Glenn that he was in love with Tisha. How could he not be? She had everything he could possibly want in a woman, partner and best friend—all rolled into one stunning and talented beauty. But he wanted to express this in words when he popped the question. Was she ready to jump back into marriage again? With him?

I sure hope so, as nothing would make me happier than to be her husband with an entire future ahead of us, Glenn told himself, as they went back to his place and kissed affectionately.

Later, Glenn and Tisha joined some of their colleagues at the Penton Club, a popular law enforcement bar on Twelfth Street and Romeo Drive, a few blocks away from the sheriff's department. Sitting around the table and

sharing pitchers of beer were Sherman Galecki, Marjorie Pierce, Rhianna Kingsley and Fritz Alvarez, to celebrate solving the Shellview County Killer murders, now
that Jimmy McPhail was dead.

Glenn, for one, wasn't necessarily in a celebratory mood.
Not with six victims dead and buried ahead of their time.
They happened to come into the viewfinder of a stone-cold
killer and paid the ultimate price. Fortunately, Jeanne had
escaped the same fate. As had Tisha, who might have been
a victim at some point, had her theory on the unsub held up.

He grinned at her and said candidly, not even wanting
to think about losing the woman of his dreams, "Glad
this is over."

"So am I," she told him, flashing her teeth nicely.
"Hopefully, everyone can take a breath now and move on."

"Amen to that." He lifted his mug of beer and clinked
hers. After what he construed as the cold shoulder from
Sherman, Glenn felt a bit guilty. He tasted his beer, got
the game warden's attention and said, "It was nothing
personal. Just doing my job."

Sherman shrugged. "It's cool." He sipped his beer and
grinned. "No harm, no foul, right?"

"My sentiments exactly," Glenn agreed.

"Yeah." Tisha patted Sherman on the shoulder supportively. "Let bygones be bygones, as the saying goes,"
she stated.

"Hey, we're all on the same page here," Fritz commented. "Getting to the heart of the issue was all that
mattered."

"And we did at that," Marjorie declared. "Jimmy
McPhail will no longer be a thorn in our sides and that's
definitely a good thing."

"I'll drink to that!" Rhianna said triumphantly, putting the mug to her mouth.

Everyone did just that, Glenn included, and then they lifted their glasses in a group toast. Though he certainly shared the satisfaction that McPhail's days as a maniacal serial killer were over and done with, Glenn couldn't help but believe that something was still missing in the equation.

What was it that was gnawing at him like a splitting headache?

Chapter Seventeen

On Monday morning, Glenn still felt something was off as it related to the Shellview County Killer investigation. Though Jimmy McPhail was presumed to be the serial killer who strangled to death six individuals and tried to murder a seventh person, it didn't quite sit right.

Yes, the indicators pointed toward McPhail, by and large, and he hadn't done himself any favors by taking his own life before being interrogated if he was really innocent. But what if he'd been made a fall guy and had actually been murdered, even if there was no solid evidence to contradict the suicide theory?

Glenn knew this type of thinking was reckless at best and downright dangerous at worst. There was no need to go against the grain in a case that had already fallen back, more or less, under the jurisdiction of the sheriff's department, where Marjorie Pierce could take much of the credit for solving the serial murders under her watch.

But I can't turn my back on gut feelings that tell me this isn't adding up, Glenn told himself, as he stood in Rhianna Kingsley's office, where he was supposed to be listening to her give him a new assignment. He didn't need to be a mathematician to know that two plus two didn't equal five or ten. How had McPhail managed to pull off multiple murders without being caught? Or identified till he risked a broad daylight attack that failed, then stole a car that was amateurish by the standards of the Shellview County Killer up to that point?

Then there was the sudden shift in the serial killer's MO, when he decided to go after Jeanne. Was this just sloppiness? A clever maneuver to throw off the investigation?

Or an indication that they were, in fact, talking about two different perps?

Could Tisha have been on to something about the link between the victims having names that derived from the name Patricia? Glenn considered the Lynda/Linda inspiration for a serial killer that criminology professor Edward Kundu was writing a book on and had brought to his attention. Convicted killer Lucas Conseco had gone after and successfully strangled eight women fatally, as his way of punishing an abusive mother named Lynda.

Had history found a way of repeating itself?

Or had it been helped to do so in the modern era?

Maybe Conseco could explain the ways and means of his homicidal tendencies, Glenn told himself. And how he was able to track, locate and kill the victims that fit the bill.

"Are you with me, McElligott?" Rhianna snapped, breaking his musing.

Glenn gazed at the special agent in charge, who was hovering over her standing desk, which was situated among other black office furniture. He was vague on the details but had picked up the gist of what she was saying. "Yeah," he muttered. "I'll be working with the GBI Human Exploitation and Trafficking Unit for my next case…going after child sex traffickers and rescuing trafficking victims…"

"Okay." Her eyes narrowed at him, as she still seemed dissatisfied. "So what's going on with you?"

Glenn sucked in a deep breath, then replied, "Something's come up."

"Care to share?" she asked.

He wanted to, but decided it was best to wait until he had more to go on, if anything at all. "Let's just say I need to tie up some loose ends…"

"On your last investigation?"

"Yeah, afraid so." Glenn met her hard gaze. "As soon as I get what I'm looking for, you'll be the first to know."

Surprisingly, she accepted this at face value and allowed him to be on his way. The rest was up to him in what would be an unusual path to take, but one that he sensed might yield some fruit.

Glenn went to his own office, where he phoned Edward Kundu, his former criminology professor. "Hey, Edward," he said, before getting right to the crux of the call. "Thought I'd take you up on your offer to help me get a face-to-face meeting with Lucas Conseco…"

"Of course, I can arrange that," the professor said. "Is this regarding your serial killer case?"

"Yes," he said flatly.

"Thought I'd heard that had been put to rest with the perpetrator's suicide?"

"I thought so, too…" Glenn leaned back in his chair. "Except for the fact that I still have a gut feeling something is off. The last attempted murder by Jimmy McPhail, the purported serial killer, deviates just enough from the other crimes attributed to the Shellview County Killer to have me second-guessing whether McPhail truly is responsible for all the deaths."

"I see." Edward paused. "But what makes you think that Conseco can be of assistance in reopening the investigation?" he asked curiously. "Or do you simply want to compare notes on one strangulation serial killer to another?"

"The latter is partly correct," Glenn confessed. "But it goes beyond that—" He explained Tisha's hypothesis on variations of the name Patricia linked killings.

"Interesting," Edward murmured.

"Assuming it is legit, with Conseco also having this in common with the Shellview County Killer, I figured it was worth a shot to see if he'll talk to me about his process of tracking down victims," Glenn said. "Maybe he can give me some insight that can either put this case to bed for good...or point me in a different direction—"

"Understood. Knowing Conseco as I've come to, I'm sure he'll be happy to explain his rationale and methods."

"Good."

"When would you like to see him?"

"This afternoon would be great," Glenn responded equably. "I can be at the prison in about an hour."

"Shouldn't be a problem," Edward said. "It's not like Conseco has something better to do with his time."

"Great."

"Good luck."

"Thanks." Glenn hung up, while believing that he didn't need luck in questioning the inmate, but rather uncovering anything that could tell him he was going on a wild-goose chase.

Or an indication to the contrary.

TISHA TEAMED UP with Sherman to give out two BUIs at Lake Oliver, then responded to the ranger hotline, where a tipster reported a poacher in a forested area of the county.

While searching for the unsub, who was thought to be hunting illegally, Tisha broke the silence between them, feeling a chill in the summertime air, as she said in a friendly voice, "So I didn't realize you'd been seeing someone…"

Sherman snorted, and responded sarcastically, "Was that before or after your boyfriend practically accused me of attempted murder?"

Tisha narrowed her eyes at him. "I thought you understood that Glenn was only doing his job in questioning you, given your proximity to the crime at the time it occurred?"

"I did—I do," he said humbly. "Agent McElligott was obligated to follow every lead. I get that." Sherman ran a hand across his brow. "Guess it still hurts a little that someone in my position with the DNR should be suspected—even for a moment—of trying to strangle a friend of yours. With the greater insinuation of being a serial strangler and murderer."

"It hurt me, too," she stressed honestly, as they made their way through tall pine trees. "For the record, I never believed you would hurt Jeanne. Much less, led a double life as the Shellview County Killer."

"That's good to hear." He offered her a crooked grin. "Anyway, it's over now and the bad guy is dead."

"True." Tisha smiled back at him, feeling as if a load had been lifted off all their shoulders with Jimmy McPhail's suicide. It made making arrests for boating under the influence or poaching pale in comparison to dealing with a callous serial killer.

"Regarding Emily, the woman I was dating, it just didn't work out," Sherman muttered. "We didn't see eye-to-eye on what we wanted out of the relationship. So I bailed. I admit, I probably could've and should've handled things a bit differently than I did."

"You're human," she said, giving him an out. "Maybe you'll fare better with the next person you date."

"I won't hold my breath on that." He snickered. "Not everyone can be so fortunate to find someone again that fits, as you have with Glenn McElligott. Could be I'm just not cut out for commitment to any one person." He shrugged. "Or maybe I am, but still searching for the woman who can win me over…"

"You just never know." Tisha flashed her teeth, pulling for him on whatever made her fellow game warden happy. At least they seemed back on track as friendly colleagues. Meanwhile, she was definitely counting her blessings in finding Glenn and being found by him, wherever this path took them.

GLENN DROVE DOWN GA-540 while wondering if speaking with the convicted serial killer would produce any results. Or if it would just be a big waste of time. It was the second option that kept him from sharing this with Tisha just yet.

Now that she had reconciled herself with McPhail being responsible for the attack on Jeanne and the serial homicides, there was no reason to throw cold water on it for the time being. Certainly as it related to intimating to Tisha that her theory on the killings had not been eliminated entirely. As of now.

I'll be happy to share what I learn, if there's anything to it that warrants further investigation of the serial murders...beyond McPhail's supposed guilt, Glenn told himself, as he turned right on GA-240 South.

A few miles later, he reached Macon State Prison on Highway 49 South, in Oglethorpe, parked in the designated area and, after locking his firearm away in the glove compartment, headed inside.

Once he got through the procedure as a GBI special agent, Glenn went to an interrogation room and waited for the inmate to show up.

Momentarily, Lucas Conseco walked through the door, wearing a khaki jumpsuit and in handcuffs. In his late thirties, he was a lean man around Glenn's height, bald-headed and clean-shaven with a noticeable scar on his right cheek.

Glenn pretended not to notice as he said tonelessly, "I'm GBI Special Agent McElligott."

Conseco peered at him with brown eyes and said, "Yeah, I know. Ed Kundu told me you were coming." The prisoner sat in a wooden chair on the opposite side of a metal table from Glenn. "But he didn't say what this was about." His brow creased. "So why don't you fill me in on why I should waste my time talking to you?"

Looks like he intends to make this more difficult than it has to be, Glenn thought, but wasn't about to be deterred or intimidated. "I'm investigating a serial killer case that's similar to yours," he told the inmate.

"How do you figure...?"

"Apart from strangling his victims, the killer has apparently targeted victims that had some variation of the name Patricia," Glenn said, and could see that this sparked an interest in him. "Given that you went after women named Lynda, I thought you might provide some insight into not so much his motivation, but how he might have gone about finding victims that were suitable for killing..."

Conseco jutted his chin. "Patricia, huh?" He pondered this for a long moment. "I like Lynda better, for obvious reasons... As for this other killer and locating the ones he wanted to find, it's not as difficult as you think—"

"Why don't you enlighten me," Glenn said, prompting him to proceed.

"Alright." Conseco took a deep breath. "Just asking around can get people talking," he said. "Next thing you know, there were more Lyndas in the vicinity than met the eye—giving me choices to pick and choose whoever I wanted. If that failed, there's always social media, where people love giving you info about themselves and how to find them, starting with their names..." He gave a little laugh. "When all that went nowhere, there was always running into a Lynda at a store, in a bar, at the hospital... or even by chance sometimes. I was patient enough to wait it out till the right person came along. Maybe this dude did it the same way," he said, speculating.

Glenn absorbed his thought-provoking take on what he did and how he did it. Perhaps the Shellview County Killer did operate the same way. He asked the convict, "Would you have ever gone after someone not named Lynda with a *y* or Linda with an *i*...maybe to try to throw the police off?"

"Nah." Conseco shook his head adamantly. "Why would I? That's not what it was all about. Wasn't in it to play games with the police, for sport, or to change my strategy just for the hell of it!"

That certainly fits with conventional wisdom, at least among criminal profilers, Glenn told himself. He also knew there were no absolutes when it came to serial killers. Was his latest case an anomaly of sorts? Or a deliberate case of diversion?

Glenn cast his eyes at the inmate and asked out of morbid curiosity, "So was it worth it—killing all those women? And for what...to spend the rest of your life behind bars?"

Conseco stared at him with a frown. "Yeah, it was worth it," he claimed. "After being betrayed by my mother over and over again, this was the ultimate payback, even if she was already dead..." He took a breath. "You wouldn't understand."

"You're right, I don't," Glenn had to admit unapologetically, "and never will. Guess it's something you'll have to live with."

"Yeah, I guess so," Conseco said defiantly. "Are we done?"

"We're done." Glenn saw no further reason to waste any more time. He wasn't sure he got what he came for. Or maybe he did in that there might not be any definitive answers that demanded the Shellview County Killer case be given another hard look. He stood up. "Thanks for the chat," he said sardonically.

"Anytime." Conseco's voice rang with equal contempt. He rose, regarded Glenn inquiringly, and said, "So what's with you special agents, anyway? Why am I so special compared to other serial killers? Or do you hound them, too?"

"You've lost me." Glenn cocked an eyebrow. "I don't follow—"

"You're the second special agent I've talked to."

"Really?" Glenn locked eyes with him. "Who was the first?"

Conseco seemed to wrack his brain and then replied, "Special Agent Kurt Stewart, I believe he called himself. Had the ID to back him up..."

Kurt? Why the hell would he have come to see him? Glenn wondered. "When was this?"

"About six months ago," the prisoner said matter-of-factly.

"What did Agent Stewart want?"

"Like you, he wanted to know all about me killing women bearing the name of my mommy dearest," he said wryly. "Why I killed them, how I found them, how difficult was it to locate them. How I managed to get away. Same old, same old." Conseco licked his lips. "Seemed just as interested in what I had to say as you, if not more."

"I see." Glenn rubbed his nose. "I suppose your unusual tale has captured the fancy of both law enforcement and true crime writers alike," he said musingly.

"Yeah, right." Conseco left the room without looking back.

Glenn's mind was racing like a thoroughbred. It wasn't lost on him that Kurt came to visit the convicted serial killer around the same time that the Shellview County Killer got started in his ligature strangulations. Why? Coincidence? Professional curiosity? Just what was Kurt up to?

Glenn didn't like at all what he was thinking as he left the prison.

Chapter Eighteen

When Glenn got home, he let Riley and his active new buddy, Jacky, run around on the property. It was his turn to take the dogs, giving Tisha a breather. This was also another example of the comfort zone they had established with one another, extending to even their furry companions. As far as he was concerned, they were all now part of one happy family. They only needed to make it official.

But at the moment, Glenn's attention was still on Kurt Stewart and what drew the special agent to pay serial killer Lucas Conseco a visit six months ago. Was his interest in Conseco related to the job? Or was his intent much more sinister?

What am I missing here? Glenn asked himself as he headed up to his office and sat at the desk. Something, like a perfectly logical explanation? *I sure as hell hope so*, he thought. He needed to find out—and soon.

Getting on his laptop, he requested a video chat with the special agent in charge of the GBI Region 6 Investigative Office, Freda Nanouk, where Kurt was currently assigned. Freda had been the special agent in charge of the Region 12 office when Glenn was working there at the same time as Kurt.

When Freda appeared on the screen, she said, "Hey,

stranger," and gave Glenn a warm smile, assuming, no doubt, that the call was more for catching up for old times' sake than something business-related.

"Hey." He smiled back softly at the fortysomething Native American, who had brown eyes and straight brunette hair in a shoulder cut, and quickly lost the smile, as Glenn said, "I need some info…"

"Okay." She gazed at him. "How can I help you?"

Glenn hated to have to go to her regarding a current special agent, but she put integrity above all else, including agent loyalty. Especially if there was any chance that the agent had gone off the rails. "I need to know if there was any reason, in particular, for Kurt Stewart to have paid a visit to a serial killer named Lucas Conseco at Macon State Prison around six months ago?"

"Hmm…" Freda was thoughtful. "No reason that I can think of pertaining to an investigation or anything. Why the interest?"

Again, Glenn hesitated, not wanting to jump the gun in accusing one of their own of wrongdoing. He explained the Patricia theory and possible connection between his latest investigation and the serial murders perpetrated by Conseco, and concluded, "Though the Shellview County Killer case has been linked to a man who killed himself, I'm not convinced that there isn't more to this story that bears looking into—"

Her brow creased. "And you think Agent Stewart could be involved…as a copycat killer…?"

Glenn sucked in a deep breath, then said in a level tone, "Until I'm convinced otherwise, I can't rule it out."

"Well, you did the right thing in bringing this to my attention, Agent McElligott," she told him squarely. "I'll certainly look into it—discreetly, of course—before pointing any fingers."

"I understand." Glenn realized she needed to go through the proper channels and procedure when it came to potentially dirty GBI agents. Unfortunately, he wasn't afforded the time for a lengthy process. Not when a serial killer could still be on the loose. And aiming to add more victims to his list of strangulation kills. Another thought occurred to Glenn. He regarded the special agent in charge and asked curiously, "Did Kurt happen to be involved in any way with Jimmy McPhail, the suspected serial killer who committed suicide as the walls began to close in around him?"

Freda's eyes widened. "McPhail was a CI in our ongoing probe into illegal gambling in the state," she responded, ill-at-ease. "So, yes, Agent Stewart would almost certainly have crossed paths with McPhail in the scheme of things…"

I was afraid of that, Glenn told himself, as he pondered this new development in connecting dots that he wished he hadn't. If Kurt was indeed a serial killer, he surely was more than capable of having made his confidential informant a scapegoat, and could have set up McPhail to escape justice himself for homicidal crimes that Kurt was guilty of.

But what Glenn couldn't figure out was the Patricia angle in lining up victims with a variation of that name. No one named Patricia came to mind that existed in Kurt's orbit, as far as he knew. So why would Kurt go through such trouble, in patterning himself after Lucas Conseco?

Had this been merely a convenient justification for the murders? Or was there some symmetry in Kurt's head to justify the murders of six innocent individuals? Not to mention the attempted murder of Jeanne, someone Kurt was supposed to care for and had been a witness to her attack.

Now, Glenn had to seriously wonder if the entire thing had been a charade on Kurt's part, with him having orchestrated the entire assault on Jeanne. And he possibly used his acumen to murder McPhail and make it appear as a suicide?

"What are you thinking?" Freda asked, snapping Glenn from his thoughts.

"That things are beginning to line up against Kurt," he told her bluntly.

"Hmm…" she murmured contemplatively.

Glenn asked, "Do you know where Kurt is now?"

"He's on an assignment," Freda answered confidently.

"Good." While still trying to put the pieces together, Glenn wanted to know that the special agent was at least temporarily preoccupied, so as to not be able to cause more trouble, if he was indeed a killer at large. Glenn leaned forward and requested, "I'd like to reach out to Kurt's ex-wife, Dixie. She may have some info relevant to the investigation—"

"Okay." The special agent in charge gave him Dixie Stewart's contact information, while he promised to keep Freda informed on where things went from there.

After ending the conversation, Glenn wasted no time in calling Kurt's former wife. He had gotten together with them a couple of times when things were still going good in the relationship. Dixie struck Glenn as a loving mother who seemed to have given it her all to keep the marriage together. Especially after they had lost their five-year-old daughter so tragically. It was Kurt who let things fall apart, with the marriage ending in divorce.

When Dixie answered the phone cheerfully with "Hi, Glenn," in seeing the caller ID, he instantly envisioned her the way he remembered the thirtysomething veterinarian as good-looking with big blue eyes behind cat-eye glasses and mounds of wavy burgundy hair, parted in the middle.

"Hey, Dixie." He tried to sound pleasant but knew that wouldn't last. "Look, this may sound like a strange question, but do you or Kurt happen to know anyone named Patricia or someone with any variation of the name?" Glenn felt this was the best way to approach the subject, without outright accusing her ex-husband of being a possible cold-blooded serial killer, who fed off a convicted serial killer to orchestrate his deeds.

"Um… Well, our late daughter's middle name was Patricia," Dixie informed him.

"Really?" Glenn was attentive. "Greta, right?" he recalled.

"Yes, Greta. But Kurt always liked to call her Pat for short, and simply because it was his special way of relating to her." Dixie paused. "Why are you asking this?"

How do I respond to that without tipping my hand? Glenn asked himself. He didn't want to get ahead of himself. Or do wrong by her by suggesting that her dead daughter may have been connected to a string of homicides in Shellview County.

"Just out of curiosity," he replied. "It was mentioned offhandedly that one of our special agents may have known someone named Patricia, similar to a name that came up during an investigation. I've been asking around, considering the irony." *I know that sounds lame and she'll probably see right through it*, Glenn thought guiltily.

"Oh." Dixie took a breath. "Greta was our little darling," she said maudlinly. "When she died, suffering the way she did, Kurt took it particularly hard. He seemed to want to blame anyone and everyone, including me." She sniffled. "Our relationship seemed to go downhill from there," she pointed out. "I gave it my best shot, but realized there was no turning back. Kurt became a no-show, both mentally and physically, for me and our other two kids. He really left me no choice but to want out of the marriage, for the sake of my family..." She stopped herself abruptly. "TMI... I'm sorry—"

"It's fine," Glenn told her sympathetically, while knowing her words carried more weight than she realized. She had unwittingly given Glenn a possible motive for Kurt turning into a killer—as bizarre as the connection seemed to Patricia. But the shoes seemed to fit, insofar as Kurt's ability to move around in plain view, his knowing the lay of the land where the homicides and attempted murder of Jeanne had occurred, and his connection to both Jimmy McPhail and Lucas Conseco. Was this enough though to make Kurt guilty? Much less, charge him and bring him in? "I wish you and Kurt had been able to work it out," he said to Dixie sincerely.

"Believe me, so do I." She waited a beat. "But it is what it is and we've both moved on, while hopefully holding on to the memories that count most—"

"Yeah," Glenn concurred. No sooner had he disconnected when a call came in from Freda Nanouk. "Hey," he answered nervously.

"I wanted you to know that Agent Stewart is not where I thought he was…"

"He isn't?"

"Looks like he called in sick, so he never showed up."

"That's a real problem," Glenn said straightforwardly, feeling his heart pounding as he passed along to her what he'd learned from Dixie Stewart about her dead daughter and how it had impacted Kurt's psyche.

When all the pieces were added together, Glenn knew that the GBI special agent had suddenly become a clear and certainly present danger.

With Tisha—another Patricia variant—in possible and probable peril.

FOLLOWING THE ARREST of the burly poacher, caught red-handed, Tisha had separated from Sherman and driven to the Manikeke Crossing, where she did some work on her computer, before heading out to track bird migration. These included hooded warblers, northern Parulas, pro-thonotary warblers and wood ducks, among others. She loved tracking their movements as part of the conserva-tion aspect of being a DNR game warden.

The fact that Glenn loved nature, too, and spending time with her and their dogs, gave Tisha that much more to find satisfaction in. She loved the man and decided it was high time she conveyed this to him and let the chips fall where they may. She hoped they'd fall right into his lap with a quid pro quo admission.

As she moved farther up into the wildlife manage-ment area, Tisha suddenly had a sense that she was being watched. But by whom? A curious animal? A hunter, taking a break while quietly observing a game warden at work?

Or none of the above?

Was this her usual overcharged imagination playing tricks on her yet once again?

Maybe, she decided, and continued with her work. No use allowing a dead serial killer to haunt her from the grave. Was there?

Jimmy McPhail was no longer a threat to her or anyone else in Shellview County. He had seen to that by taking the coward's way out of facing true justice for his horrendous actions. This came too late to save Tris Lindberg and the other poor victims from dying by his wicked hands.

But Jeanne had been spared from a similar fate. Thanks in large part to Kurt coming to her rescue, just in the nick of time. How fortunate it was that he happened to have made plans to meet up with Jeanne at the very time that McPhail decided she was an easy target.

Could McPhail have been that dense or desperate so as to suddenly decide to go after Jeanne randomly in a much more visible setting than with his other victims? Even to the point of trying to strangle her with his bare hands, in a distinct change of course?

How was that even possible?

Especially given the craftiness the perp had exhibited when handpicking his other victims for his signature ligature strangulation. And before managing to get away without detection, much less being taken into custody.

Yet this was apparently exactly what happened.

Tisha wanted to question this. But to do so would mean that the case had come to a close prematurely. That the killer was still out there. And on the prowl for victims, just as they let their guard down.

Just stop it, Tisha admonished herself, as she moved

deeper into the woods. She didn't want to look for trouble that wasn't there. Not when there were so many positive things in her life right now that she should be focusing on.

When her cell phone rang, Tisha removed it from her uniform pocket, and smiled when she saw that it was Glenn calling. No doubt to make dinner plans for the evening. Or even breakfast in the morning.

But before she could respond to the call, Tisha heard some footsteps from behind her, and a familiar voice that commanded, "I wouldn't answer that if I were you, Tisha—"

She turned around and her heart skipped a beat as Tisha saw Kurt Stewart standing there, glaring at her. In his hands was what she recognized to be a Ruger-built Marlin Model 336 Classic .30-30 lever-action rifle, and he was aiming it at directly and menacingly at her.

Chapter Nineteen

Glenn was disturbed that Tisha failed to pick up her phone when he called to warn her about Kurt and her being a possible target of the special agent, now suspected of being a serial killer.

Had she been prevented from doing so? Or was she otherwise too preoccupied to answer her cell phone?

Sensing it was more likely than not the former set Glenn into near panic mode. The thought that Kurt would go after Tisha was worrying, to say the least. All things considered, he sure as hell wasn't about to leave it to chance that Kurt's thirst for death had ended with the ligature strangulation of Patrice Whitney.

And possibly the murder of Jimmy McPhail.

Not in a million years.

Or even a trillion years.

Not when Tisha means everything to me, and so much more, Glenn told himself. He loved her. Dearly. Losing Tisha would rock his world and destroy everything they were heading toward as a couple. Including starting a family. He couldn't allow this to be taken away from them.

After getting the dogs, Glenn loaded Riley and Jacky into the back of his SUV, before the three of them headed out. With his cell phone on the dashboard mount, he put it on speakerphone as he called Sherman Galecki.

Sherman answered immediately. "Agent McElligott…" he said tentatively.

"Hey," Glenn began, realizing that there were still some tender feelings there after interrogating the game warden as a suspect in the attack on Jeanne. "I need to find Tisha. Do you know where she is right now?"

"Yeah. She's in the Manikeke Crossing, tracking bird migration." Sherman paused, then asked instinctively, "What's going on…?"

"Tisha could be in danger," he told him without prelude, while heading toward the WMA. "I think the Shellview County Killer is still alive."

"What?" Sherman's tone rose with shock. "But I thought Jimmy McPhail had been identified as the killer…?"

"I thought so, too." Glenn peered at the road. "It looks like McPhail may only be guilty of attacking Jeanne Rutland."

"So who are we talking about here as the serial killer culprit?" Sherman's voice broke as if the finger was again pointed at him.

"I strongly suspect that GBI Special Agent Kurt Stewart is the killer," Glenn told him straightforwardly.

"Seriously?" Sherman muttered an expletive. "I remember talking to Agent Stewart at one of the crime scenes. I thought he seemed smug, but never imagined this."

"Trust me, neither did I." Glenn sighed. "Can't really go into the details right now. I just need to make sure that Tisha is safe. I've been unable to reach her by phone. Maybe you can try?"

"Of course. If I can't connect with her, I'll alert the

work section sergeant, Fritz Alvarez, to send out a search party to the Manikeke Crossing."

"Alright."

"We'll find her," Sherman said, trying to reassure him.

"We'd better," Glenn snapped with more force than intended as he disconnected, then put on the speed, fearing that every second counted if he were to save Tisha.

TISHA NEEDED A moment to come to grips with the situation she found herself in, as she stared down the barrel of a rifle that Kurt aimed at her while wearing black gloves. It obviously wasn't good. "What is this…?" she demanded of the special agent, who was wearing an orange hunting vest over a flannel shirt and jeans.

"Just what it looks like, Tisha," he said, stone-faced. "I'm holding you at gunpoint." He jutted his chin. "Now, why don't you ditch the phone for starters, please…"

She hesitated, knowing it was her lifeline to the outside world. To Glenn, in particular, who had called and would know she didn't—or couldn't—pick up to respond.

"Do it!" Kurt demanded sharply, then warned her, "And don't even think about turning your body cam on!" He glared at her threateningly. "Toss your phone my way—"

After she threw the cell phone to the ground near his feet, Tisha watched as he slammed his hiking boot onto it several times, rendering it inoperable, while never taking his eyes off her.

"Now, the gun, Tisha," he ordered. "Remove it slowly with your left hand and drop it—"

Tisha wanted desperately to reach for her Glock pistol, secure in its holster. Not to do as he wanted. But to use it to defend herself. Should she give it a go? Was she quick enough to hit him before he could shoot her?

"I know what you're thinking..." Kurt chuckled daringly. "I don't doubt that you know how to use that firearm. But in this instance, I'd advise you to not even try. I can assure you that in a battle to see who's quicker to the trigger, you'll lose. So do as I tell you, or die trying, right now!"

Unwilling to hedge her bets in putting this to the test, Tisha again did as she was told in using her left hand to remove the gun and placed it on the ground.

"Now, back up," he ordered her, which she did, and he moved forward and grabbed her firearm with one gloved hand, while keeping the other aiming the rifle at Tisha squarely.

As Kurt tucked her firearm in the front of his jeans, she glared at him unnervingly and stated, "Never took you for a what...kidnapper, rapist, or—"

"Try serial killer," Kurt boasted, watching her stunned reaction. He added, "Or shall I use the tried-and-true familiar moniker, the Shellview County Killer..."

Tisha's eyes widened as what he was indicating registered. "You?"

"Afraid so," he said gloatingly. "The cat's out of the bag, so to speak—at least for you."

"And why is that?" Tisha asked, even as she processed what he was saying and what the big reveal meant for her getting out of this alive. If that was even possible, with him holding all the cards.

"Heard through the grapevine that you'd figured out the Patricia connection to the killer," Kurt pointed out. "Patricia was actually the middle name of my dead daughter, Greta. For the record, though, my special nickname for her was Pat. I don't mind telling you, seeing that you'll never get to reveal this to another living soul."

Tisha was shocked to learn that there was a link to the name variations after all. Had Glenn been able to piece it together somehow? Did he even have a clue that she was now a prisoner of his fellow special agent friend, who clearly intended to kill her, too?

"You killed six innocent people because of your late daughter?" she asked, in trying to make sense of this.

"Yeah," he confessed. "I went after them in honor of my little Pat, who never got the opportunity to grow up to live the lives they did. As far as locating suitable victims, it wasn't all that difficult to find some with other versions of her middle name. In the case of Walt Patrick, it was entirely coincidental that his surname happened to be a male form of Patricia, as it was actually his girlfriend, Patti Arnaz, that I targeted. And in case you're curious about how I managed to kill an Australian with a version of Patricia as her name, well, Patrina Morse introduced herself to me during a hike, which proved to be quite fortunate for me and not so much for her."

"That's sick!" The words spurted out of Tisha's mouth, in spite of being at a disadvantage to the killer. "How could you, as a member of law enforcement, do such a thing?" She recalled that Sherman had once been in the same situation, only to prove himself innocent. That obviously wouldn't happen here.

Kurt laughed, while keeping the rifle steady in front of him. "You'd be surprised just what law enforcement personnel are capable of, should the circumstances warrant bad behavior. This was such an occasion. But that doesn't mean I was willing to cut my own throat. I planned this, without making it too obvious, so as to ruin my own life any more than it already had been ruined—with Pat's death, ending my marriage, and losing custody of my other kids. The way I saw it, why should these other females get to grow up and enjoy adulthood when Pat couldn't? So unfair—"

And so insane, Tisha told herself, hating to think that Jeanne had gotten involved with a homicidal maniac. He had clearly succeeded in pulling the wool over Glenn's eyes, too, in wanting to set them up. If only they had been able to see through Kurt for the monster he truly was. Had Jeanne begun to see the light, even after he appeared to be her savior?

Kurt's jaw set as he said musingly, "I'm sure you're wondering where Jeanne fit into the equation as a victim. Well, she was only meant to be a distraction—to throw off the investigation and any notion that the victims were connected by their names. I coerced my confidential informant, Jimmy McPhail, to attack Jeanne, but not hurt her badly. He was supposed to use all my tricks of the trade, including the stun gun and cord, to pretend to strangle her. Unfortunately, the idiot forgot to bring the cord and had to rely on his hands to put around her neck...before I conveniently came to Jeanne's rescue."

Tisha wrinkled her nose and snorted, "You're unbelievable." She knew that he was truly much worse than that. Jeanne deserved so much better than to have aligned herself with a fraud and killer.

"Maybe I am." Kurt gave a humorless laugh. "But for what it's worth, I actually like Jeanne and intend to continue seeing her, once you're out of the picture, Tisha, as one final offshoot of Patricia in my daughter's memory."

Tisha recoiled at the thought of meeting the same fate as his other victims. Even if he was changing his methods for the kill. Being shot to death instead of strangled was hardly a picnic that she wanted any part of. So how could she fight back, before there was no fight left in her?

"Start walking," he demanded, using the rifle to point deeper into the forest. When she hesitated, he said coldly, "Or you can die, here and now, and that will be it. Your choice."

Knowing that there was only one choice—give herself a fighting chance—Tisha complied with his order. She began to head toward the trees, where sounds became muffled, and one could easily get lost to the point of disappearing entirely. Was that his intention?

"Did McPhail really kill himself?" she asked out of curiosity and to buy her precious time.

"In a manner of speaking." Kurt chuckled. "He signed his own death warrant by botching the job, giving Glenn reason to believe it might not be the same perp that killed the others. Truthfully, McPhail had to go, any way you sliced it, as someone who could tie me to the attack on Jeanne. And, by extension, the Shellview County Killer. So I lured him to a spot, where I used a ghost gun I'd confiscated from a crime scene, shot him with it, then planted the weapon in McPhail's hand." He snickered. "Worked like a charm, if I say so myself!"

What a jerk, as well as psychopath, Tisha told herself, more than a little worried that he would be successful in his dastardly plans for her. She turned her head, while continuing to walk into the woods, and growled, "You're never going to get away with this."

"You think?" Kurt asked, mocking her. "Watch me.

You'll be shot accidentally by a hunter, who will never be found. Since the Shellview County Killer case was already resolved with the death of Jimmy McPhail, your death will be entirely unconnected to the serial killer investigation. While I commiserate with Glenn over his loss, over a beer or while playing basketball, I'll be home free. So, yes, I'm pretty confident that I will get away with ending your life, Tisha, with Jeanne by my side all the way."

He laughed sardonically, as though believing himself to be untouchable and able to continue hiding his maniacal character from everyone.

Though Tisha would like nothing better than to wipe that smug grin off his face, trouble was, she wasn't exactly in a position to wrest that rifle away from him, while they were further apart than arm's length to try and grab the barrel. Not without the real risk of getting shot, and probably never being able to show her love for Glenn and the amazing life they could have together.

And so she waited for the slightest crack in the rugged armor of the GBI special agent turned serial killing fiend that would allow her to fight for her life…without necessarily dying while trying. With the clock ticking, one second at a time.

During the drive, Glenn phoned the sheriff and said, "There's been a new development in the Shellview County Killer case—"

"Really?" Marjorie responded.

He relayed to her what he suspected about Kurt, providing just enough specifics to make his case, and listened as she gasped with incredulity, before Glenn said abruptly, "On the off chance that Stewart actually took a legitimate sick day, you should work with the Baldwin County Sheriff's Office and send deputies to his house in Milledgeville."

"Count on it," she assured him. "We'll get a search warrant as well. If Agent Stewart truly is our serial killer, he's likely to have kept evidence in his safe space."

"I agree." Glenn also requested and was promised backup as he neared the Manikeke Crossing, not wanting to leave anything on the table in locating Tisha.

Lastly, he called Rhianna, filling her in on everything, knowing the special agent in charge should have been the person he brought this to first. Except for the fact that with time being of the essence, he needed to kick things into gear as quickly as possible in achieving the best results.

Rhianna, who was understandably distraught with the news that a GBI special agent had become the primary suspect as a serial killer, promised her full support in bringing this to a close, however it went down.

"Bring Agent Stewart in," she commanded unflinchingly.

"I fully intend to," Glenn told her determinedly. "One way or the other."

Upon reaching his destination, he let the dogs out and rendezvoused with Sherman, who was standing in the parking lot near Tisha's empty Ford F-150. "Help is on the way," he told Glenn reassuringly.

Though happy to hear that, it wasn't nearly soon enough for Glenn's comfort. "Can't wait around while Tisha is out there, perhaps injured…" He couldn't bring himself to say dead. "Which direction is she likely to have gone to track the bird migration?"

Sherman contemplated this and answered, "My guess

is that she would have headed toward Harlin's Creek—"
he pointed in that direction "—where they're most active
at this time of year."

"I'll check it out with the dogs," Glenn told him. "We
should split up to cover more ground, till others arrive—"

"I agree." Sherman met his eyes. "I want to find Tisha
safe and sound as much as you do."

"Thanks." Glenn nodded, appreciating his fondness
for her as a great game warden. He headed out, and said
urgently to the dogs, "Let's go find Tisha—"

With Riley and Jacky leading the way, Glenn made his
way through trees, shrubbery and streams, while hoping
against hope that he could reach Tisha in time, if she was
in harm's way…but then he noticed that the dogs were
circling something on the ground. He caught up to them,
and asked curiously, "What you have there?"

He saw that the red-colored object in question was a
cell phone, and picked it up, recognizing it.

Tisha's phone.

It had obviously been damaged beyond repair, and not
likely by Tisha.

Kurt must have her, Glenn told himself. Or hurt her.
His heartstrings pulled at the thought, as he surveyed the
landscape in search of Tisha.

Just then, Jacky and Riley bolted, as if picking up Tisha's scent. Glenn followed them, struggling to keep up,
while removing his SIG Sauer handgun.

When he caught sight of Tisha—still alive, thankfully—being forced to move through the woods by Kurt,
who was holding a rifle on her, Glenn knew that this was
crunch time. He needed to distract Kurt in order to pre-

vent him from shooting Tisha, before taking down the crooked special agent.

Without a second to spare, Glenn told the dogs, who were already on the move, "Get him!"

As they raced to protect Tisha from a very bad guy, Glenn took aim at Kurt, knowing that in this instant, there was no room for failure.

"THAT'S FAR ENOUGH," Kurt told her snippily, once they were deep enough into the wooded area to satisfy him.

Tisha turned around tensely to face the serial killer, who was still aiming his rifle at her. "I hope you rot in hell!" she snapped, meant mainly to get a reaction, before she made a desperate attempt to come out of this alive.

He laughed at her mockingly. "I'm sure I will. Too bad you won't be around to spit on my grave."

As she contemplated his ominous threat and saw her life flashing before her eyes, Tisha saw Jacky and Riley racing through the woods to get to her—and him—before it was too late, with Glenn in hot pursuit. Though she tried to avert her gaze, Kurt caught her eye movement and looked in that direction.

He turned the rifle toward the dogs. Knowing she couldn't let him shoot Jacky or Riley, in a split second, Tisha lunged at Kurt, forcing the barrel of the rifle down as a shot went off and hit the ground.

Putting into practice the self-defense techniques she'd learned, Tisha used her knee to hit him as hard as she could in the groin, while simultaneously striking the killer in the throat with the palm of her hand. As Kurt doubled over in pain, but still managed to hold on to the rifle, Jacky flew up in the air and clamped her teeth around his wrist. As Kurt howled, he let go of the rifle, just in time for Riley to jump on him, propelling both to the ground.

The serial killer was kept at bay until Glenn arrived and pitched in with a solid blow to Kurt's jaw, then slapped cuffs on the man. "Did he hurt you?" he asked Tisha, concern in his eyes, as Jacky licked her cheeks affectionately after coming to her rescue with Riley.

Tisha glanced at her bloodied, moaning assailant and answered comically, "I think it's more the other way around."

Glenn chuckled as he looked at the fallen foe. "Yeah, seems that way."

"With a little help from my furry family," she added, as Jacky and Riley circled her, clearly proud of their efforts to avert disaster.

"It seemed like a good idea to bring them along while searching for you, and let them have at him when push came to shove."

"How thoughtful of you." Tisha smiled gratefully. "Didn't hurt the cause any for you to contribute a nice crushing blow as well in putting a stop to Kurt's deadly intentions toward me."

Glenn acknowledged this, as he stated, "Happy to help. Believe me." He then glared at Kurt and asked with asperity, "Just tell me why all this? And why go after Tisha, in particular?"

As he struggled to maintain consciousness, Kurt sighed and responded callously, "They all had to die as versions of Patricia, because with my daughter Pat's illness, she never had the chance to reach adulthood to be like them someday…" He cast a wicked gaze at Tisha, and hissed, "She had the misfortune of also having a name variation of Patricia—so she had to die. You have to know that it was nothing personal toward you, Glenn…"

"That's where you're dead wrong, Kurt," he growled. "It was very personal to me. Maybe someday you'll come to realize that while you spend the rest of your miserable life behind bars!"

Kurt grumbled before passing out as Sherman came upon the scene. He approached them, eyeing Tisha. "You okay?"

"Yeah." She smiled thinly, glanced at Kurt and back. "Have to admit, though, for a while there, it was pretty much touch-and-go. Agent Stewart fully intended to do me in and make it look like a hunting accident. Or a stray bullet that just happened to have my name on it."

Sherman wrinkled his brow. "That wasn't going to happen," he argued. "Agent McElligott had your back every step of the way. So did I." He gazed at the dogs. "Guess they did, too."

Tisha watched as Jacky and Riley stared intently at him, clearly still in defense mode. "Thanks, Sherman," she told him with a sheepish grin.

"Just glad you're all right." Sherman regarded Kurt, who was coming around, then turned to Glenn and said, "Sorry it had to be a GBI special agent who went rogue."

"No more than I am." Glenn glared at Kurt. "But he'll be held fully accountable for everything he did, as would anyone else in society who broke the law as a serial killer and—" Glenn met Tisha's eyes endearingly "—attempted murderer."

Sherman nodded. "Good to know."

Tisha concurred, casting her eyes from Sherman to

Glenn. "The important thing is that this seems to finally be over, for all of us and Shellview County—"

Almost on cue, deputies and other law enforcement personnel arrived and Kurt Stewart was placed under arrest and led away from Tisha and Glenn, and the crime scene of a planned attempted execution.

Glenn moved to Tisha and the dogs, who still seemed very protective of her, and said regretfully, "I wish we'd been able to figure out his madness and menace sooner."

"Me, too." She wrapped her arms around Glenn's rigid waist. "But it's truly over now. Kurt confessed to it all, and his warped sense of honoring his daughter's memory as a serial killer. Including setting up Jimmy McPhail to attack Jeanne and take the fall as the Shellview County Killer; before killing him and making it seem like suicide."

"I'd gathered as much," Glenn told her, holding her close to his body. "Kurt was inspired by the serial killer I told you about, Lucas Conseco. I paid him a visit earlier today at Macon State Prison, and he enlightened me about receiving a visit six months ago from Kurt and giving him the skinny on his modus operandi and means for tracking down his victims."

"Wow." Tisha's brow creased. "Definitely two peas in a pod."

Glenn laughed humorlessly. "Yeah, that's one way of looking at it. Now, Kurt will have the opportunity to join Conseco in prison, where they both belong."

"You'll get no argument from me there," she assured him, pulling away and standing on her tiptoes to give Glenn a kiss. "For a minute there," she admitted, "I wasn't sure I'd get the chance to do that again."

"The thought crossed my mind once or twice, too," he

confessed. "But together, we made sure that wasn't the case. Instead, we'll have plenty of time to enjoy each other's kisses."

"Promise?" Tisha gazed lovingly into his gray eyes.

"With a cherry on top!" Glenn said amusingly, and kissed her again, then said, "Let's get out of here."

"I'm all for that. And so are Jacky and Riley." The dogs barked simultaneously to that effect.

Tisha felt Glenn's fingers interlock with hers on one hand and, looking beyond her official statement on her ordeal to give to the DNR, GBI and the sheriff's department, welcomed the opportunity to spend precious time with those she cared about most.

Epilogue

A week later, Glenn was still counting his blessings that Tisha had been unharmed physically during her dangerous encounter with Kurt Stewart at the Manikeke Crossing. Knowing that the deranged, at least in some respects, serial killer had set his sights on Tisha as the supposed final victim of Kurt's rage against society in losing his daughter made Glenn all the more grateful that Tisha had lived to see another day.

If he had anything to do with it, that would stretch into many, many days, months, weeks and years, where he could cherish her with everything he had. And if he could get back even half as much, it would definitely make him one extremely happy man.

They were sitting on the couch in Tisha's living room, eating takeout Chinese chicken chow mein with bamboo chopsticks, with the dogs dining on their own food, when Tisha broke into Glenn's thoughts, as she asked, "So what do you suppose Kurt's ultimate fate will be? Will a good lawyer with the help of a capable psychiatrist be able to use some sort of insanity defense to try and get him an eventual get-out-of-jail-free card?"

Glenn weighed this for a moment or two, while eating, then he replied, "My guess is that any attempts to somehow mitigate his guilt will fall flat. Courts these days

tend to frown upon defense strategies based on the perpetrator unable to distinguish right from wrong in justify-
ing heinous actions. One need not look any further than
Kurt's mentor, if you will, in Lucas Conseco. Beyond
that, given the ball of cotton rope found at Kurt's place
that corresponded with strands found on the victims—not
to mention a DNA match with one of the victims found
on a section of rope that he apparently used to strangle
her and failed to dispose of—and a treasure trove of cir-
cumstantial evidence found on Kurt's laptop, it's pretty
clear that there was willful intent on his part to commit
the murders, while concealing his guilt. Hardly what you
would call someone not playing with a full deck."

She nodded agreeably above her chopsticks. "You
know, I was thinking the same thing. Crazy behavior can
only go so far when choosing to end lives for some con-
voluted rationale."

"Right?" Glenn agreed thoughtfully. "I just hate that
Kurt's ex-wife and children will have to bear the burden
for his homicidal actions and the dead bodies left in his
wake."

"Me, too." Tisha scooped up some noodles. "Also, it's
so sad that Jeanne thought she had a potential keeper in
Kurt. Only to find out that he was anything but someone
she wanted to start a romance with."

"At least she lived to talk about it," Glenn pointed out.
"Though Kurt had Jimmy McPhail do his dirty work for
him—with a little more pressure around her neck or the
stun gun being applied to the wrong part of Jeanne's body,
the result could have been far worse for her."

"I know." Tisha ate food ponderingly. "I'm pretty sure
there's someone out there for Jeanne, worthy of however
long it takes for her to want to go back down that road."

"Yeah, definitely." Glenn met Tisha's eyes solidly. "Just like there's someone in here for me...and you—"

She fluttered her lashes boldly. "Oh, really?"

"Absolutely."

"Well, I have to admit, I think you're wonderful, Glenn."

"Is that so?" He smiled askance. "Right back at you, Tisha...and then some."

"Hmm..."

Glenn took that moment and said to her, "Uh, I think you've got a little bit of chow mein on your chin—" Just as she was about to wipe it away with the back of her hand, he checked her, and said smoothly, "Allow me."

He leaned over and kissed her perfect chin, following this with a kiss on the lips, then declared, "All better now."

"Nice to know. So clumsy of me." Tisha blushed and puckered her lips. "Shall we try that cute trick to kiss me again...?"

"Got me." Glenn laughed guiltily. "Absolutely. Let's go for it."

"You'll get no disagreement from me," she promised.

As they went for a longer, tastier kiss, Glenn found himself wanting more than ever to finally tell Tisha how he truly felt about her. Yet he held back, knowing he needed only a few more days to be able to make the announcement perfect for what it meant toward their future. He only hoped they were in sync in that regard.

For now, he was happy to settle for running his hand through Tisha's long hair and kissing the most gorgeous, sexy and on-top-of-her-game woman in the world.

ON SATURDAY, Tisha sat on Glenn's deck, beside him, as he played his guitar. Jacky and Riley were lying there lazily, liking the soft music, and perhaps the satisfaction of having their owners together, enjoying each other's company.

Tisha had hoped that by now Glenn would have expressed his feelings more for her in words, though his adorable actions were quite affectionate. She decided that now might be a good time to tell him exactly how she felt about him and what she wanted more than anything—a second chance at love and to be his wife and the mother of his children. Would this pull them closer together? Or push them apart?

As she contemplated this, Tisha took note that Glenn had started to play and sing at the same time, the 1920s classic romantic tune, "It Had to Be You," recorded by such artists as Billie Holiday, Frank Sinatra and Harry Connick Jr.

Mesmerized by the words, Tisha flashed her teeth and wondered where this was leading as Glenn stopped midway through, put the guitar down, took her hands and uttered soulfully, "It has to be you for me, and only you, Tisha."

Her heart nearly melted. "Really?"

"One hundred percent." He peered into her eyes. "I've been sitting on this knowledge for a while now, waiting for the right time to tell you how I felt about you… I'm totally and deeply in love with you, Tisha—and I want you to be my wife…" Glenn released one of her hands and pulled out from behind him a yellow double halo 1.2 carat diamond engagement ring, wrapped in platinum. After falling on one knee, he slipped the ring onto her finger, and it fit perfectly, then he asked, "Will you marry me, Tisha Fletcher, and make this GBI special agent the happiest man on the planet? Not to mention, Riley would love to have you as his adopted mother…and hopefully we'll have some human kids to add to the family down the line…"

"Yes, yes, yes, and as many yeses as it takes," she blurted with glee, while admiring the ring and then the handsome man himself. "I love you, too, and will marry you, Glenn McElligott! And I'd be honored to adopt Riley and give Jacky a canine sibling to have fun with for a lifetime." Tisha chuckled as Jacky barked, in giving her wholehearted approval. "And as for children, I love the thought of being a mother, with you as their doting father."

"Thank you!" Glenn beamed as he straightened back up. "I can hardly wait to make this a reality," he declared.

Her eyes lit. "Neither can I."

"How do you feel about honeymooning in Alaska?" he asked expectantly. "My sister would love that and they'd give us an amazing place to bring our families together. Or if you'd rather have a honeymoon in Hawaii, Europe, Asia, or the Caribbean—"

"I'd love to have our honeymoon in Alaska," Tisha insisted. "That would be so incredible! There will always be other occasions to vacation in Hawaii, Asia, Europe, the Caribbean, or anywhere else we choose to visit."

"Very true. Anywhere at any time. As long as we're together—forever!"

"Absolutely," she replied, seconding his words enthusiastically.

A big grin played on Glenn's handsome face, as he cupped her cheeks and planted the biggest kiss on Tisha's mouth. She reciprocated in kind, as she loved kissing him every chance she got, while knowing there would be much more of this to look forward to for years to come.

* * * * *